MURDER IN LAVENDER SILK

A BRIDAL SHOP COZY MYSTERY

KAREN SUE WALKER

*M*ax Walters awoke with a smile on her face It was the eve of her thirtieth birthday, and tonight her boyfriend, Detective Jason Cruz of the Crystal Shores Police Department had a date planned for the two of them. He hadn't shared the details, but she knew it would be special.

She hummed happy songs while she showered and got ready for work. The moment she stepped through the back door of her father's home, she smelled the invigorating aroma of freshly brewed coffee. She could always depend on her dad to put a pot on to brew the night before, and it was one of the bonuses of living in the apartment over the garage. This was the same kitchen where he let her try coffee for the first time at the age of eight. He put plenty of milk and sugar in it and Max's love of coffee was born.

When her mother had found out, she had scolded him, and Max knew at that moment that even though she loved both her parents, her dad was the fun one. That didn't prevent her from still missing her mother who'd passed away four years earlier.

With a fresh cup of coffee, she went to look for her father. Richard Walters would either be in his studio or still asleep. As a freelance artist, he didn't have to punch a timecard, but older people like him seemed to be early risers. He was almost sixty, after all.

She found him in his studio, a converted sunroom. He sat in front of a painting with his back toward her, his paintbrush aloft as if undecided on his next brushstroke. Perhaps the piercing black eyes of the woman on the canvas had transfixed him. Max felt as if she'd interrupted a private moment. She quietly took a step back, meaning to slip out before he noticed her presence, but the floor creaked and he turned around.

"Oh, hello, Sunshine," he said with a tired smile.

"I didn't know you were doing portraits again. It's been a while."

"Yes, it has." He glanced at a framed painting of Max's mother that hung on the wall before returning his gaze to the mystery woman.

"Who is she?" It wasn't prying when it was your own father, was it?

Richard pulled a cloth over the painting. "I'm working from a photograph," he said, gesturing to his computer.

On the screen she saw a photo of the dark-haired woman, wrapped in a brightly colored shawl similar to one her parents had brought her back when they'd returned from vacation years ago. "Is she South American?"

"Bolivian," he answered. Before she could grill him further, he asked, "Are you hungry? How about pancakes?"

Darn it. Her dad sure knew how to distract her.

THE WIND WHIPPED MAX'S HAIR IN EVERY DIRECTION AS she hurried to her shop. The charming seaside town of Crystal Shores was rarely warmer than seventy-two degrees, which Max considered to be the perfect temperature, but today it had to be at least eighty and it wasn't even ten o'clock. Plus, it was December! A bit late for the Santa Ana winds that arrived to heat up southern California every fall, but hopefully the heat wave would ease in time for her to wear some of her Christmas sweaters.

Wedding Belles Bridal Shop would be a cool, air-conditioned oasis of calm, at least until the first client arrived.

Nestled among the shops, bakeries, and restaurants that lined Coast Highway, Wedding Belles was popular with brides from all over southern California who appreciated a boutique experience over a big, impersonal chain. Brides often made a day of it, following their bridal fitting with lunch at a charming local café like Chez Mer, browsing the exotic floral displays at Flower to the People, and ending the day with a stroll on the beach. The town of Crystal Shores was a hidden gem, sitting as it did between Laguna Beach, favorite of artists and tourists, and Newport Beach, with its multi-million-dollar homes and yachts.

She'd worked at Wedding Belles since her teens, and except for two years when she'd apprenticed for a top design firm in New York, the shop had been like a second home to her. Two years ago, she'd jumped at the opportunity when the owner offered to sell her the business. At the time, she'd prepared herself to work long hours, but she hadn't expected it to take over her life the way it had.

Stepping inside the doors of her shop, Max took a deep breath. Her former boss used scented oil diffusers, but so many people had sensitive systems that Max quit using them. That's when she discovered that wedding gowns had a smell all their own, and it combined deliciously with the subtle scent of the sea that drifted in every time the door opened.

After putting her purse away in the office, she tried taming her shoulder-length wavy hair, but brushing it only made it frizzier. She settled for a ponytail. It would do for now.

"Max?" Keiko called out from the back room. "Is that you?"

Max had hired Keiko three years ago as her assistant, and Keiko had become indispensable. Each morning, Max looked forward to seeing what outfit Keiko had picked out. Whatever trend she might be following, it was never boring. She found Keiko on the floor of the sewing room in a frilly pink dress surrounded by fabric scraps. "You're here early. What in the world are you doing?"

With her pigtails and sheepish look, she resembled a child bracing for a scolding. But under the lace and ruffles, Keiko was as strong as Alpaca fiber. "It seemed like a good idea when I started. We have so much left-over fabric I decided to purge."

Oh, dear. Purge had become Keiko's favorite word. In spite of handling the shop's website and social media, plus helping out with clients on busy days, she found time to organize.

"Not again," Max teased.

"You would prefer that I allow everything in this room to take over until there is no room to even move in here?"

Max thought that was a bit dramatic. "If that happens and I get stuck in here, will you bring me snacks?"

Keiko ignored her, and instead held up swatches of silk and lace. "Some of these pieces are less than a yard. Not even enough for a bodice. Perhaps we could sell them online, make a few dollars, and free up some space. A win-win."

"Sell my cabbage?" Max said a bit louder than she meant to.

"Cabbage?"

"It's an old-timey term from when everyone's clothes were hand made. The tailor or dressmaker got to keep the excess fabric as a sort of a perk."

"But why do they call it cabbage?" Keiko asked.

"No one knows for sure. There are lots of theories, even one that tailors liked eating cabbage, but that just sounds silly if you ask me." Max grabbed a piece of fabric from Keiko. "This is from Fiona's granddaughter's christening dress. And this..." She pulled another remnant from the pile on the floor. "This is from Tiffany's dress, the first wedding gown you designed." Keiko and Max had worked together to create the unique, leather-trimmed gown, and it had brought in more referrals to the shop than any other single gown.

Keiko's brown eyes widened. "How can you possibly remember that when I can't even tell one from another?"

Max shook her head slowly. "I don't know. I guess I've just spent a lot of time with these fabrics." She sighed. "I suppose they're not doing any good taking up space in a box. But I hate to get rid of them."

The front door jingled, and they said in unison, "Heidi."

Their new assistant called out, "Hello, anyone home?"

Max left Keiko with her piles of fabric and headed into the showroom, so she and Heidi could begin preparing for a busy Saturday.

Once Max had admitted she and Keiko couldn't run the shop alone, it took months to find the right person to hire. Heidi worked in retail before taking a few years off when her two children were born. She loved everything about the bridal business, which she'd learned all about by watching reality TV.

Heidi was relatively prompt, organized, and didn't seem to mind being bossed around by Keiko. Keiko enjoyed having someone to boss around, even if she pretended to be annoyed at the seemingly endless questions Heidi asked.

"What kind of lace is this?" "Why do we have so many buttons?" "What color is peridot?"

Keiko would sigh and give Max a long-suffering look before answering. Keiko always had an answer and only rarely did she make it up. On these occasions, Max would turn around only to see Keiko shrug while suppressing a grin.

The front door jingled again as Eric Mancini, owner of Flower to the People and one of Max's best friends, entered. In his arms, he held a large box wrapped with silver wire and greenery.

"Happy birthday." He put the package down on the coffee table.

Max regarded the exquisitely wrapped present eagerly. "Wow, it's gorgeous. Can I open it now?"

"No. Your birthday isn't until tomorrow."

"I know that," Max said. "Aren't you coming to my birthday brunch?"

"I'll be working. We're doing the flowers for a wedding at the Montage in the afternoon, plus a fifti-eth-anniversary party tomorrow evening, and my usual delivery driver is on vacation. I'll be finishing up the bouquets and floral displays plus driving the van."

"Can't Daphne cover for you?"

Eric rolled his eyes dramatically. "Not if I still want

to have a business by Monday. She's even more distracted than normal with the wedding coming."

"You need to find a new assistant, Eric." Max couldn't count how many times she'd told him this.

"Not everyone can find someone like Keiko," he said.

"And me!" Heidi piped up. How long had she been standing there?

"Yes, of course," Eric said, with unusual restraint. "And you."

"What kind of plants are those?" Heidi pointed at the sprigs entwined in the silver wire.

"Ruscus and jacobaea maritima, commonly known as silver ragwort. Don't touch it."

"Why, is it poisonous?" she asked.

"No, I just don't want you to touch it."

"It's charming," Heidi said.

"Thank you," Eric said coolly. Charming was one of Heidi's favorite words and indicated her highest approval rating, but Eric considered his taste to be classic and elegant, and preferably very expensive looking.

He turned back before he got to the door. "How's Daphne's dress coming?"

"Fine," Max said. It would be fine if the fabric she'd ordered would ever arrive. "You will be able to come to my dad's opening on Thursday, I hope." Max's father Richard had procured a gallery showing of his newest works.

"I'll do my best to be there."

"You better," Max said.

"Or what?" Eric winked and closed the door before she could threaten him with some dire consequence she would never carry out.

Heidi appeared behind her. "I'm afraid I can't make it to your father's opening. I'm so sorry, but my kids—"

Max held up a hand. When Heidi started talking about her young children, she often included more details than Max wanted to hear. There might be spitting up babies and diapers to change in her future, but not anytime soon. "No explanation necessary. Let's just get to work, shall we?"

CHAPTER 2

*O*ne bride's mother and her maid of honor nearly came to blows before Max found a gown everyone could agree on. Another bride spent an hour and a half trying on almost every dress in the shop until the time allocated for her consultation was up. When Max suggested scheduling a second appointment, she admitted she liked the first dress she tried on best. Max smiled through clenched teeth and reminded herself as she took the young woman's deposit that everyone had a different way of making sure they made the right decision.

Her four-thirty appointment showed up on time with her mother, twin sister, and future mother-in-law. Alexis Brussel was a referral, so Max expected her to have high expectations and hoped she would be open to guidance. Brides usually knew what they thought they wanted, but often didn't know what would look best on them. That was certainly the case with Alexis.

Max took one look at her newest client and realized that the blush gown she wanted to try on wouldn't compliment her coloring, but Alexis would have to figure that out for herself with a bit of help. Alexis picked out a stunning princess gown with a skirt comprised of layers and layers of chiffon.

Alexis slipped into the gown and Max could feel her excitement as she led her to the room that she called the Dream Room to show everyone her first choice. Her family stopped talking as soon as she entered.

Alexis stepped onto the pedestal. "What do you think?" she asked, smiling tentatively.

Mrs. Brussel spoke first. She managed to say, "Oh, well--" before Alexis' sister Alana piped up.

"No way! I'm not letting you go down the aisle looking like the walking dead. You look positively gray."

Alexis sucked in a breath but didn't respond. She turned to her future mother-in-law. "What do you think?"

"It's pink," she said.

"Yes," Alexis said. "Well, blush, actually."

"You should be wearing white."

Alexis ran from the room, and Max followed her. She was used to unsupportive family members who cared more about what they wanted than what the bride wanted, but Max happened to agree that blush wasn't the right color for Alexis. She just wouldn't have put it as bluntly as Alana had.

"She's horrible. She always has been," Alexis said as Max unzipped the dress and helped her climb out of it.

"You mean your sister?" Max asked. "She's a bit blunt, but maybe horrible is a bit strong of a word, don't you think?"

Alexis gave her a contrite look. "Maybe so." She sat down on the chair in the dressing room, looking deflated. "I don't know if I want to try on any more dresses today. Maybe another time. Maybe without my fiancé's mother. I don't want this to turn into a battle of wills.

Max's thoughts went to Jason's mother, who Jason had promised she would meet soon. Mrs. Cruz had three sons, and Jason said she couldn't wait for her sons to marry so she could finally have daughters.

"Does your future mother-in-law have any daughters?" Max asked.

This brought a smile to Alexis' face. "No. She always says I'm the daughter she never had. She asked me to call her Gigi, because that's what she wants her grandchildren to call her someday." Alexis blinked a couple of times, and Max held out a tissue box for her to wipe her eyes.

"How about this?" Max suggested. "Do me a favor and try on one more gown. If I'm right, we're going to need a lot more tissues."

"I don't want a white dress," Alexis protested.

"It's not white," Max said.

"I don't want off-white either. Or ivory, ecru, bone, cream—"

"Just wait here," Max interrupted. She slipped out of the dressing room and returned moments later with a silk gown. She pulled off the protective plastic cover and held it up for Alexis to see.

"It's purple," she whispered.

"Lavender," Max corrected. "A lovely, pale lavender." It really was a beautiful shade, and Max had been waiting for the right bride to wear it. "It's the new blush, didn't you know?" She gave Alexis an encouraging smile.

Alexis gazed dreamily at the dress. "It's gorgeous. Can I try it on?"

Max laughed. "I think that's the whole point, don't you?"

"But what if they hate this one, too?" the bride-to-be asked as Max helped her into the gown.

Max calmly replied, "Then I suggest you take your family to lunch and make sure they have a few drinks before you bring them back."

Alexis grinned. "I might just do that."

The silk off-the-shoulder gown complemented her skin tone perfectly, and the ruched bodice showed off her curves. Yards and yards of delicate silk flowed to the ground and pooled behind her.

Max could almost feel Alexis holding her breath as she made her way back into the Dream Room, the skirt swishing softly as she walked.

Alexis' mother simply stared as if speechless.

"You look beautiful!" her sister said, breathlessly.

Alexis' future mother-in-law scowled. "It's not white," was all she said.

"It's lavender, Gigi," Alexis said hopefully.

Max gave her a wink. "Leave it to me," she whispered.

Keiko perked up when she saw Max step into the showroom and grab a veil from the display.

"Show time?" Keiko asked, and when Max nodded, Keiko grabbed a few hair clips and followed Max back into the other room.

As Alexis stood facing the mirror with her back to the others, Keiko put her hair up into a simple twist and clipped on the floor length veil. Max draped it over her shoulders.

"Ready?" Max asked, and Alexis nodded.

Alexis turned around and the room was quiet except for the sound of her mother and sister sniffling as they wiped away happy tears. Keiko rushed to pass the tissue box around. Max held her breath as she tried to read the mother-in-law's tight-lipped expression. Was she humming?

"It reminds me of that song," Gigi said, and she softly sang, "Lavender blue."

"Dilly dilly," Alexis finished the phrase.

Gigi began blinking back tears, which was clearly a losing battle. "Who cares if it's not white? You look like a dream."

Alexis squealed with delight and jumped off the podium to hug everyone, starting with Gigi.

Once Max had taken the deposit and the women

had left, she slipped into the office and plopped into an easy chair. She called out to Keiko, "Please tell me that was our last appointment." She'd lost track.

"Yes, it most certainly was." Keiko locked the front door and turned the sign around, so it showed they were closed.

Max looked over her shoulder at the wall clock. "It's not six o'clock yet."

"Close enough." Without saying a word, she walked past Max into the office at the back of the store. She reappeared with a feather duster and began attacking the display cases holding tiaras and veils with it. Luckily, nothing was fragile.

"Are you in a hurry or something?" Max felt guilty sitting watching Keiko work, but it felt so good to sit down. "You don't have to do that. I'll take care of it after I rest for a minute. I'm exhausted."

"Of course, you are. You work twelve-hour days, seven days a week."

A noise from upstairs startled Max, and then she remembered Heidi. Max had sent their assistant to the second floor to organize the newly arrived stock. She reluctantly gave up her comfy spot and headed toward the back of the shop.

"Heidi?" she called out. A moment later, Heidi appeared at the top of the stairs, her sandy hair pulled up in a messy bun, which was not how she'd started out the day. "You can come down now."

"Thank goodness!" Heidi clomped down the stairs

panting. "It's really stuffy up there." She wiped a damp strand of hair off her face.

"You should have told me," Max said.

"I don't like to complain. But it was really hot. And stuffy."

Keiko reappeared. "You already said that. What were you doing up there?"

"Organizing. And steaming the wrinkles out of the dresses." She scowled at Keiko, and then went to get the vacuum cleaner.

"They're gowns," Keiko corrected her needlessly.

"What's gotten into you?" Max asked Keiko. "Are the Santa Ana winds making you grumpy?"

Heidi rolled the upright vacuum cleaner up to them. "It's the positive ions."

Keiko said, "What?"

"The Santa Ana winds create positive ions that affect your mood. Ironically, not in a positive way." She turned the vacuum on and began running it up and down the colorful rug that covered most of the showroom floor.

"What time is Detective Cruz picking you up?" Keiko asked over the drone of the vacuum.

"In less than half an hour," Max answered. "And you can call him Jason, you know." When Keiko didn't respond, she added, "I told him I needed time to close up the shop."

"But really, you need time to get ready."

"Well, of course," Max said. "After all, we haven't been able to have a date night for two weeks. Plus, with this crazy wind," she pulled the scrunchy out of her ponytail, freeing her frizzy mane, "I need to do something about this."

Keiko slipped into the office and returned with her tote bag. "Want me to fix your hair?"

Max grinned. "That would be awesome."

Keiko regarded Max's conservative business attire. "Do you want to change first?"

"Yes, I brought jeans and sneakers."

Keiko shook her head disapprovingly.

"Jason said to dress casually," Max explained, not sure why she felt defensive.

Keiko sighed. "That just means wear flats and bring a sweater."

"It does?"

"Yes. Why does every other woman know that except you? Jeans will be fine, but no sneakers. Luckily, you wore ballet flats today. It gets cold as soon as the sun goes down—do you have a sweater?"

"Yes..."

Keiko tilted her head to one side. "You're not taking that ratty old thing on your date tonight."

"You helped me pick out that ratty old thing, as you call it. I love it."

"And you've worn it every single day since you bought it." Keiko went into the office and returned with a beautifully wrapped box with a huge pink bow. "Happy birthday!"

"Thank you, Keiko, but my birthday isn't until tomorrow."

"I know. But you need this now."

That piqued Max's curiosity. She began to carefully peel back the wrapping paper.

"What are you doing?" Keiko said impatiently. "Just rip it off."

Max laughed and did as she was told. She opened the box and peeled back tissue paper, revealing a black silk bomber jacket with pink trim and embroidered accents. Max turned it over in her hands, admiring the beautiful details. "Did you make this?"

"Yes," Keiko said tentatively. "It's machine embroidery, of course. I know it's not your usual style—"

"I love it!" Max exclaimed.

Keiko beamed. "You really do? You're not just saying that?"

"Let's face it. My personal style tends to be a bit boring. I've been trying to be a more adventurous with my wardrobe, but I haven't had any time to go shopping." Max took a closer look at Keiko's handiwork. "The workmanship is beautiful. "

"I learned from the best."

Max grabbed Keiko in a hug, which startled Keiko, but she permitted it, even patting Max on her back a couple of times.

Once Keiko had finished transforming Max's frizzy mop into a beautiful French braid, the office phone rang. Max jumped up and rushed to answer it.

"If he asks, will you say yes?" Keiko asked. Max tripped over an armchair, which made Keiko erupt in a fit of giggles.

"Did you move that?" she asked as she reached for the phone, but Keiko just laughed harder.

Keiko stopped laughing when Max returned from the office with a frown on her face. "Oh, no."

"Oh, yes," Max said. "Something came up at the station. He has to work late." She sighed. "You'd think I'd be used to it by now."

Heidi appeared behind them. "That's terrible! And here we thought he had something special planned for later tonight. I can't believe—"

"I'm sure you want to get home to your family, Heidi," Keiko interrupted.

Heidi put a hand on Max's shoulder. "I remember what it was like to be without a date on Saturday night. I don't mind staying around if you need someone to talk to."

Max ignored Keiko's snicker, which turned into a cough. "Thanks, that's very kind, Heidi, but you should go home to your family."

Heidi grabbed Max in a sudden hug and then collected her purse and was gone.

"Well, I don't have any plans for tonight," Keiko said. "I'll take you out for a drink."

"Where? It's Saturday night. Every place will be jammed."

"We'll go see Burt at the Crazy Fox," Keiko suggested. "He'll feel sorry for you and get us a spot."

Max put her hands on her hips. "Are you calling me a loser?" She tried hard to keep a straight face, but she couldn't hold back from giggling.

"It seems as though we are both losers tonight. Come on, slowpoke."

"A slowpoke and a loser," Max mumbled as she retrieved her purse from the office, and then she brightened. "Hey! You're only young and single once, right? Let's go have some fun!"

They stepped out onto the sidewalk, just as the holiday display in the center divider lit up. Topiary dolphins covered in twinkling lights led Santa's sleigh.

"I never understood how dolphins are supposed to take the place of reindeer," Keiko commented.

"They're magic dolphins," Max explained.

Keiko eyed her doubtfully. "That makes all the difference then."

CHAPTER 3

*I*t seemed as though everyone in town was at the Crazy Fox tonight, and Max and Keiko could barely squeeze past the crowd gathered just inside the door waiting for a table. They found their way to the cocktail lounge, where Burt waved to them from behind the bar with one hand as he maneuvered a martini shaker with the other.

"Where's Burt supposed to squeeze us in?" Max asked Keiko. Every bar stool was taken, and the dozen or so tall tables were also full.

"No worries, Max," Burt said. "I've got you covered. The weather's so warm, we opened up the back patio as a second cocktail lounge. Check it out. I think you'll like it."

Keiko grabbed her elbow and guided her toward the back of the restaurant.

As they walked past the bar, Max overheard a

woman's voice at a nearby table. "I hate this town. So much money and so little taste."

Max turned to see the source of the comment and stopped in her tracks. The woman looked exactly like the woman in her father's painting. The only thing missing was the shawl. Instead, she wore an elegant silk jacket draped over her shoulders.

Keiko tugged at her arm. "What are you looking at?"

Max turned back to Keiko. "My father is working on a painting of a woman. That woman." She discretely pointed out the woman. "If that's not her, then she's got a doppelganger."

A man wrapped an arm around the woman's shoulder. "Come to Milan with me, Eliana," he said. "You will love it there."

"As soon as I'm finished with the attorneys, and the insurance, and selling the house, I'm going home to South America." She added flirtatiously, "Perhaps you would like to come visit me there."

"Come on," Keiko whispered. She led her down a hall past the restrooms, paused at the back exit, and pulled opened the back door. "After you," she said, and gave Max a little push into the dark outdoor patio.

Max stood blinking, trying to get her bearings when the lights came on, momentarily blinding her.

A chorus of voices yelled, "Surprise!"

She looked around the festively decorated patio at all the smiling faces and turned back to Keiko. "What's going on?"

Keiko smirked. "Have you never heard of a surprise party?"

She looked at the faces again and realized they were all her friends and neighbors. "A surprise party? For me?"

Jason appeared in front of her, and she thought her heart might stop beating. He was dressed casually for a change, and he looked just as handsome as the first time she'd met him, with his dark hair and mesmerizing green eyes. She felt like the luckiest girl alive to have him for her boyfriend.

"You look beautiful." He handed her a glass of champagne and gave her a quick kiss.

"I'm so glad you're here," Max said. "I thought you had to work late."

Jason laughed. "Yes, I was hard at work hanging up streamers and lights. Richard's a slave driver. I didn't want to lie to you, but it was for a good reason, don't you think?"

Max looked around the room and squealed when she saw her best friend Olivia, who rushed to greet her. "You said you weren't coming back to town until next week." The two embraced in a long hug.

"I hope you'll forgive me for not telling you I came back yesterday," Olivia said. "Eric told me you've never had a surprise party, and we thought it was about time. As a bonus, we figured we'd get you to spend some time with all of us."

"Yes," Eric said, appearing at Olivia's side. "You have been spending much too much time at that shop of yours. Besides, this is a big one. Tomorrow, you're going to be—"

"Twenty-nine," Olivia said, cutting him off.

Max spotted Fiona by the buffet table and waved, and the older woman came to join them.

"It's okay," Max said. "You can say thirty. There are worse things than getting older, you know."

"Yes," Fiona said. "It beats the alternative. Happy birthday, Max. I want you to enjoy the last day of your twenties, but you should know that the best is yet to come."

Max happily sipped her champagne as she walked around the room saying hello to everyone.

"Hungry?" Jason asked, but before she could answer said, "Never mind, silly question. Your dad talked to Burt and ordered all your favorite appetizers. I'll go check on them."

Max looked around at the twenty or so people at the party. "By the way, where is my dad?"

"Good question," Keiko said.

The room seemed to go quiet, and Max turned to see what everyone was looking at. She blinked as if she were seeing a mirage.

It was Eliana, the woman from the painting she'd just seen in the restaurant. What was she doing here at Max's party?

Richard appeared beside her, and held out his arm, which she took. He leaned closer to tell her something, and the gesture and her smile were so intimate, Max knew that her father hadn't told her everything about this woman or his relationship with her.

He took his eyes off his date and called out to his daughter. "Max! Happy birthday! I'm so sorry to be late." He hugged her and stepped back to introduce his date. "This is Eliana Baldassari. I just ran into her in the restaurant and asked her to join the party. I hope you don't mind."

Eliana nodded as she was introduced to Keiko and Fiona.

"And this is my daughter, Max."

Max stared at Eliana but forgot to say anything. Her eyes were even darker than in the picture.

Keiko pinched Max's arm. "Ouch."

"Sorry," Keiko said. "You know how you get when you haven't eaten." She turned to Eliana. "She goes into a sort of trance. I'd better get her something to eat. Nice meeting you."

"Yes," Max said. "Nice meeting you."

Max followed Keiko to a table where Jason stood and pulled out a chair first for her and then for Keiko.

"Thank you, Detective Cruz, but I think I will go and get Max another drink."

Jason leaned in close to Max. "How do I get her to call me Jason?"

"Stop intimidating her," Max suggested.

"What? I didn't do anything."

Max laughed. "I know. But for some reason, you make her nervous. You always have."

Keiko returned with a specialty martini. "Here. Burt made it just for you. It's purple."

"I can see that," Max said.

"You like purple."

Max couldn't argue with that logic, so she gave up and took a sip. "Oh my, that's delicious. What is it?"

"I think he called it an avatar," Keiko said. "No, an avatation? An invitation? I forget."

"Never mind," Max said. "Sit down a moment, would you?"

Jason's phone buzzed. "I'll be right back."

As soon as he was out of earshot, Keiko said, "What is going on?"

"I just wanted to thank you. This is awesome."

"Your dad did most of the planning," Keiko said. "But I meant what is going on with your father and that woman. Are they dating?"

"Not that I know of. He said he was painting her from a photograph." Max took another sip of the drink to fortify herself. "Did you see her eyes? They're black as night."

"That's a bit dramatic, don't you think?" Keiko stood up. "She is very beautiful. I will say that."

"My dad thinks so, obviously." She watched him from across the room. "He can't take his eyes off her."

Jason reappeared by her side. "That's a good thing, right? I mean, it's not like anyone could replace your mother, but don't you want your dad to find someone?"

"Yes, but," Max began, but couldn't think of a good way to end the sentence.

"Look," Keiko said. "I forgot to get a drink for myself." She gave Max a thumbs up and headed for the bar.

Jason leaned closer. "I'd rather talk about us," he whispered in her ear.

"Us?" Max felt his warm breath on her neck and her skin tingled. Was everyone right? Was he going to propose?

Before Jason could say more, Eric sat down across from her. "Are you having a good time? Do you need another drink?"

"Keiko just brought me one," Max answered. "By the way, who's paying for all this?"

"That is none of your concern, young lady," Eric said. "Your job is to have a good time. And I don't want you two sneaking out early."

Keiko reappeared with two more drinks, one for herself and one for Max. This one was cherry red. "Here is another for you to try. Before you ask, I don't know what it is called either."

"But I haven't finished the purple one," Max said.

"It's your birthday," Keiko said. "Taste this one and whichever you like the least, Eric will finish."

"What?" Eric sounded terribly offended. "I don't—" he began.

"Just kidding," Keiko said. "But I'm sure it won't go to waste."

Jason's phone buzzed again, and he tried to noncha-

KAREN SUE WALKER

lantly look at the screen. "I'm sorry, Max, I have to take this."

"No problem." Max nervously watched him walk toward the alley to take his call. Was she ready to get engaged? They'd only been dating for six months, but they'd known each other much longer. She knew he was a good man, and she knew he loved her. What else did she need to know?

More people arrived including an old friend from design school and her old boss Darlene and her husband. She spent the next few hours catching up with old friends and being waited on hand and foot.

Later that night, she noticed her father sitting at a table talking to some people she didn't know, and Eliana wasn't with him.

"Would you come with me?" Max asked Keiko. "I want to talk to my dad."

"And you need me for backup?" Keiko raised her eyebrows.

"Just come, please." The two of them made their way over to Richard.

"Hi, Sunshine," Richard said. "How are my two favorite entrepreneurs doing tonight? Are you having a good time?"

"Yes, great." Max didn't know how long it would be until Eliana returned, so she got right to the point. "Are you and Eliana an item?"

"We're friends," he said, smiling indulgently.

"Just friends?" Max asked.

"You're so suspicious," Richard said. "If we were dating, why would I hide it from you?"

Keiko spoke up. "But you obviously really like each other."

Richard took a deep breath. "She's Mrs. Leo Baldassari."

"Oh." Max recognized the name at once. His paintings were everywhere, in prints, and postcards, and t-shirts. The originals went for five figures or more.

"She's married?" Keiko asked, looking confused. "Who is Leo Baldassari?"

"I'm surprised you've never heard of him," Max said. "He was a very successful painter—called himself the Painter of Brilliance."

Keiko grimaced. "The Painter of Brilliance? That's a bit much, isn't it?"

"He died in a plane crash off the coast of Mexico," Richard said. "Just four months ago."

"Oh, that's right." Max remembered hearing about it but couldn't recall the details. "I had forgotten all about it."

"Eliana was devastated, as you might imagine. You know I didn't always get along with Leo, but I did respect his marketing skills."

"Yes, and no wonder," Keiko said. "The Painter of Brilliance. Why didn't you think of that?"

Her dad, along with plenty of other artists in the community, had accused Baldassari of selling out. But while the others said it behind his back, Richard had said it to his face. Baldassari's comeback was that amateurs often made those sorts of claims about successful artists.

Max saw Eliana heading their way, and Keiko excused herself. "You're on your own," she whispered.

Eliana must have noticed Max's sheepish look. "You've been talking about me, haven't you?"

"I'm so sorry for your loss. I can only imagine how devastated you must have been."

"You can do more than imagine," Eliana said. "You and your father both. He lost his wife, but you lost your mother. And at such a young age. That's why Richard's been such a help to me. After a few months, most people think you should be done grieving."

Her words went right to Max's heart. "You never stop grieving," she murmured.

Eliana smiled and blinked a few times. "You're so young and yet so wise."

Max shrugged. "Not wise so much but been there." She added, "And tomorrow I'm turning thirty, so not all that young either."

They were interrupted by the sound of a clinking glass and turned to see Eric tapping his champagne flute with a knife to get everyone's attention.

"Thank you everyone for coming to our soirée for our dear Max," he began. "What can I say about Max?"

Whatever he intended to say about her, Max would have to wait to find out, because several restaurant patrons chose that moment to stumble out the back door and into their private gathering.

"Hey, look, it's a party," one of them said, slurring his words.

"Dude," another said, addressing Eric, "why weren't we invited?"

A tipsy redhead tottered behind them on stiletto-heeled sandals. "I know you." She pointed straight at Max. "People are always dying around you." She turned to the two men. "Get me the hell out of here."

CHAPTER 4

The room was silent for a moment and then everyone began speaking at once. Jason reached the trio quickly and escorted them back into the restaurant, perhaps planning to make sure they weren't driving home.

The next moment, Olivia took Max's arm. "Let's get some fresh air." She led Max out the back to the alleyway.

Max glanced back at the patio, where the party had quickly returned to full swing. "Did you hear what she said?"

"Don't pay any attention to that," Olivia said. "Some people can't hold their liquor."

"Is that what people think of me?" Max asked.

"No one who counts."

Max couldn't get the woman's words out of her mind. "People *are* always dying around me," she said quietly.

"It's not like it's your fault," Olivia said in her most reassuring voice. "Let's give it a few minutes for things to get back to normal, and we can slip back in."

"Thanks, Olivia."

"I've missed you," Olivia said with a smile. "Can I take you to lunch tomorrow?"

"I'm not sure. My dad's taking me to brunch, and I need to catch up on some work at the shop."

"On your birthday?" Olivia said. "You need to take a break occasionally."

Max took a long breath in and let it out slowly before she spoke. "Do you think anyone would be upset with me if I went home? I'm really tired."

"Do you want Zach and me to give you a ride?" Zach was Olivia's husband.

"There you are," Jason said, appearing around a corner. "Why do people think that drunks are fun? Half the calls we get in this town are about drunks, either being obnoxious or trying to get in their cars to drive home."

"That's good, isn't it?" Olivia said. "I mean, it's better than half your calls being about stabbings or drive-by shootings."

"I suppose you're right," Jason agreed. "So why are you two spending Max's party in the alley?"

Jason put his arm around Max's waist, and something about the small gesture made her feel safe.

"I think Max has had enough for one night," Olivia said. "Now that you're in good hands, I think I'll track down my husband." She hugged Max, and told her,

"Happy birthday." She turned to Jason. "Take care of my best friend, Detective."

"Will do," he assured her.

When they were alone, Jason took her chin in his hand and gazed into her eyes. "You do look tired. Want me to walk you home?"

Max felt her knees go weak. It happened every time he looked at her like that. "Yes, please."

They walked to the end of the alley and turned toward her street.

Jason cleared his throat. "I had something I wanted to ask you but maybe it's not the right time."

So, this was it. Would he be angry if she asked for some time to think it over? More likely he would be disappointed. Did she need time? She loved him and they got along great. Why wouldn't she say yes? It's just it was so soon. "Well, you can ask me anything. I mean, I don't always have the answer, but I..."

"Maybe it would be better if we talk tomorrow when you're not so tired," he said.

"No, now that you've brought it up, I'd really like to know what's on your mind." If she didn't find out what he had to say now, she wouldn't sleep a wink.

Jason paused and took a deep breath before he spoke. "How would you feel about moving to Florida?"

"Huh?" That was the last thing she expected him to say.

"I haven't officially been offered the job yet, but my former chief has asked me to head the homicide division in Miami. It's an amazing opportunity. A lot more money, but that's not the most important thing. It could lead to even better things."

"Uh-huh." Max could barely speak. Instead of proposing he was considering moving away?

"Is that all you can say? I'm thinking about the future. Our future."

Max stared at him for a moment. What was she supposed to say? "You're leaving? Moving back to Florida?"

"I haven't made a decision yet."

"And what about me?"

Jason smiled and for the first time since they had met, she wanted to smack him. "Have you not been listening? I hoped you'd come with me."

"You mean, you want me to move to Miami and what? Live together?"

Jason took both her hands in his. "If you're not ready to move in with me, you can stay with my mother. She has a huge house and I know she'd love to have you there. We can figure the rest out once we get settled. I love you, Max. I want us to be together. I just don't think we should rush into anything."

Max had lived in New York in her early twenties and after she lost her mother had passed up the chance to return to the Big Apple to be a fashion designer. Her friends and family were more important to her than climbing the ladder of so-called success, and it had turned out to be the best decision she could have made. It was only a little more than two years ago that she'd bought Wedding Belles Bridal Shop from her former boss, and business was booming. She had built a life here—a good life.

She stared down the street at the rows of cozy cottages with their neat little gardens. The street where she had grown up, gotten her first job, and learned to sew. This was her beautiful town, her home. She took a deep breath, inhaling the salty ocean air that she loved so much. "I don't want to move to Florida."

He let go of her hands. "Not even with me?"

"I have my business, my dad, my friends. Everything I love is right here."

"I thought you loved me?"

"You know I do. But if you loved me, why would you ask me to give up everything so you can do what you want to do? And besides," she felt her adrenaline kick in, "you don't even like Miami."

"I never said that. Miami's great. Coming here was a career gamble, but it's paid off. And it gave me a chance to get away from the big city for a while."

"So, coming here was like an extended vacation?" Her voice rose to a higher pitch as it always did when she got angry. She took another deep breath to calm herself, not wanting to say anything she'd regret later. "You could have told me that sooner."

"I didn't plan it this way. I didn't plan to fall in love."

She avoided looking at him while she willed herself not to cry. Life was like that. Just when you thought things were getting good, someone or something would sucker punch you, leaving you gasping for breath.

After what seemed like a long time, he spoke up again. "Can't we talk about this? Why don't you just take a trip out there with me? You can meet my mother. She's going to love you. We can take the red-eye Saturday night and come back on Monday, so you won't have to close the shop."

Max realized they were standing in front of her father's house. "I need to get some sleep," she said.

"Okay." The disappointment in his voice was impossible to miss. "We can talk tomorrow."

Max walked around the side of the house to the back and climbed the steps to her apartment. She felt numb and didn't want to think about what Jason had asked her and what it meant. Not right now.

CHAPTER 5

*H*er phone rang as soon as she got home. Olivia. She almost let it go to voice mail, but at the last moment picked it up.

Olivia's voice sounded excited. "Did he propose?"

"No, he didn't." Max told Olivia everything, barely holding back tears.

"Let me get this straight," Olivia said when she'd heard the whole story. "He wants you to move to Miami and leave everything behind, but he didn't ask you to marry him? What a jerk."

"Oh, don't say that." No matter how much her heart hurt, Max knew Jason was a kind, caring person. He just saw things his own way. "I just don't think he understands the choice he's asking me to make. And even if he asked me to marry him, I don't want to leave everyone and everything that's important to me."

"In that case, I suppose it's better he didn't propose,"

Olivia said. "That would have been an even bigger dilemma."

They talked for a while longer until Max felt exhaustion take over her body. She crawled into bed and fell right to sleep.

When Max woke up the next morning, she decided to focus on her business and put everything else out of her mind. She had plenty of work to keep her busy.

Ever since her former boss Darlene had opened Wedding Belles Bridal Shop over two decades ago, custom, one-of-a-kind gowns had been a big part of their business. With her artistic skill, design skills, and expert craftsmanship, Max had made a name for herself, and custom gowns had become a lucrative part of their business.

The problem for Max was that it was not easy finding seamstresses with the necessary skills and availability. The one seamstress she'd relied on for the past year had stopped by in person a week earlier to let Max know she wouldn't be taking on any more projects.

But since today was Sunday, and it was her birthday, she'd worry about finding another seamstress tomorrow. Her father had promised to take her to her favorite brunch spot at the beach, so she dressed in shorts and flip flops, looking forward to a walk on the sand later.

Max stepped through the back door, which opened into her dad's kitchen, and called out his name.

"I'll be ready in a minute," he called back.

She poured herself a cup of coffee and sat down at the kitchen table to wait for him. Her phone buzzed and she saw a text from Jason. *Happy birthday. Can I see you later?*

She replied, *Thank you,* and thought about what else to write. She finished with, *I'll be at the shop later,* and hit send.

Her father interrupted her thoughts. "Ready to go?"

It was a glorious day at the beach, just the right mixture of warm sun and cool breezes. They found a table on the wooden deck and ordered mimosas. When the drinks arrived, Richard raised his glass.

"A toast. To my beautiful, talented daughter. I can't believe it's been thirty years since I first held you in my arms. You have brought nothing but joy to my life." He held his glass out to touch hers.

"Thanks, Dad," Max said, "though I'm not sure how accurate that is."

He grinned. "I'm pretending your teenage years didn't exist."

They ordered beignets and brioche French toast with a side of bacon for Max.

"Is Jason taking you to dinner?" Richard asked.

"He has to work. That's why we were going out last night for my birthday. At least I thought we were."

"You know," Richard smiled. "Fiona thought he was going to propose to you last night. She was quite disappointed when I told her you'd gone home." He paused. "I suppose if he'd proposed after the party, you would have told me."

"He asked me to move to Miami with him," Max blurted out.

Richard seemed taken aback by this. "But he didn't ask you to marry him?"

"No, he said I could live with his mother until, well, I'm not sure what. He said we'd figure it out later, or something like that."

"And what did you say?" Richard asked.

"I don't want to leave you and my friends, not to mention my home and my business. It was just so sudden. I still don't know how I feel about it. But I know I don't want to move to Miami. At least not now."

"Not without a ring on your finger."

Max smiled at her father's old-fashioned ideas. But he had a point. If Jason wasn't ready for a real commitment, then why should she give up everything to follow him all the way across the country?

The server put their plates down, which gave Max a brief reprieve from talking about her personal life.

When she finished the last bite of bacon, she leaned back in her chair, feeling like she'd never want to eat again. "Why did you let me order all that food?"

Richard chuckled. "I guess that means you don't want the last beignet?"

Max frowned. "I hate for it to go to waste." Funny how she never thought twice about cauliflower going to waste. Beignets were a different matter.

She wanted to ask him about Eliana, but she wasn't sure how to bring up the subject. Getting to the point usually seemed like the best way. "Dad?" she began.

"Yes?" He raised his eyebrows and waited for her to continue.

"Are you dating Eliana?"

He smiled indulgently. "No, we're just friends. I was acquainted with her and her husband before he died. Leo and I didn't see eye to eye on a number of subjects. I ran into Eliana a month or so ago, and she seemed to appreciate having me to talk to. I think I've been able to help her through her grief."

"Since you've been through the same thing," Max said.

After a barefoot walk along the beach, Max asked her father to drop her off at the shop. He started to give her a lecture about working too many hours, but when she reminded him she was a grown adult, he shrugged and said, "Just don't work too late."

###

The sewing machine whirred as she sewed, and when she let up on the presser foot, she heard pounding on the front door. She stepped into the showroom and saw Jason looking through the glass with a huge bouquet of white roses.

Max let him in and took the bouquet, burying her face in the fragrant blooms. "They're beautiful and they smell absolutely heavenly. Thank you."

Jason waited while she retrieved a vase, and when

she returned, he suggested they go out for ice cream. "It's not the same as the fancy dinner I wanted to take you to, but I couldn't get the evening off."

"You don't have to explain," she said. "I'm glad we get to spend a little time together, at least. And I'll take ice cream over an expensive steak anytime."

Jason grinned. "I'll keep that in mind."

They walked along Coast Highway holding hands and looking in the shop windows. Max pulled him into the local bookstore. She browsed the shelves while he picked out a cookbook for his mother and a collection of Agatha Christie stories for Max.

"If you're going to keep solving mysteries," he said, "you might as well get some tips from Miss Marple."

They finally made it to the ice cream shop, and Max ordered a double cone with chocolate fudge and rocky road.

"You really do like chocolate, don't you?" he teased.

Max gave him a questioning look. "There are other flavors?"

Jason laughed. "I've heard rumors there are flavors like vanilla and strawberry."

"Sounds like one of those crazy conspiracy theories to me," she replied with a smile.

By the time they got back to the shop, Max had almost forgotten that Jason wanted to move thousands of miles away. When he kissed her and said goodbye, she wondered if they would soon be saying goodbye forever.

The rest of the week flew by as Max ran her business, spent evenings sewing, and put feelers out for a new seamstress or even better, two. She looked forward to the second half of December, when the shop would be quiet, but after New Year's, she'd most likely be busier than ever. A lot of engagements happened on Christmas and New Year's Eve.

Thursday came around before she knew it, and after another busy day at the bridal shop, it was time to support her father at his first big Laguna Beach gallery show.

"I can't believe we're late." Max waited so Keiko, with her platform shoes clunking on the sidewalk, could catch up. "I had no idea parking would be such a pain. I've been to Laguna on a Saturday night before, and the crowds usually stick to the downtown area. I've never seen it this busy south of the canyon. I wonder if there's some sort of event tonight."

"Yes," Keiko said as they turned the corner onto Coast Highway. "Actually, I believe they are all coming to the gallery."

Max stopped in her tracks. A huge line snaked down the block from the far corner almost to where they stood.

"Wow." Max pulled out her phone. "I knew Dad had lots of friends, but this is an amazing turnout. I'll text him. I hope we don't have to wait like everyone else."

A woman at the end of the line turned and glared at her.

"Oops." Max fought the urge to explain that it was

her father's show as she sent her text. "Someone must be doing some great marketing."

"That would be me," Keiko admitted proudly. "I've taken over your father's social media. He now has over fifty thousand followers."

Max stared at Keiko. "That's really good, right?"

Keiko gave her a look of incredulity, and once again, Max felt left out of the loop. "How many followers does our shop have?"

"Wedding Belles is up to a couple of thousand."

"That's all?" Max was a bit disappointed, even though they had a steady stream of business.

Keiko pouted, but she didn't say a word.

"I mean… that's great!" Max corrected, hoping she hadn't offended Keiko.

"You can't handle the work you have already," Keiko complained. It was definitely not the first time she'd said that.

"Girls!"

Max looked up to see her father heading their way wearing a huge grin. He hugged both of them, his blue eyes sparkling. Max couldn't remember when she'd seen him look so happy, at least not since her mom died four years ago.

"You've got quite a turnout," Max said.

"Thanks to Keiko," he responded.

Keiko bowed her head humbly. "I only gave your art the audience it deserved. All these people are here to see your artwork."

"And to hear about the big announcement you've been teasing," Richard added.

Max looked from Keiko to Richard as they chatted, feeling a bit left out. What announcement? Before she could ask, Richard waved them to follow him to the entrance.

A burly doorman let them in the front door of Hildalgo Gallery into a wall of people. A silver-haired man in an elegant, brocade jacket rushed toward them waving his arms. "No, no, no! You must not let anyone else enter. The fire marshal will close us down." A striking young woman with short dark hair followed him in impossibly high heels.

"But—" The doorman began.

"Max," Richard interrupted. "You remember Xavier Hildalgo."

"Richard, I didn't see you there." Xavier's demeanor changed immediately, and he became the gracious host. "Max, come in, come in. Lovely to see you again," he gushed and gave her a kiss on each cheek. Max smiled at his pseudo-European manners and accent, since, according to her dad, he'd grown up in Philadelphia. He turned to the dark-haired woman. "Andrea, get Max and her friend some champagne. This is a celebration."

"Right away, Mr. Hidalgo." Andrea hurried away.

He turned to Keiko. "And who is this delightful creature?"

Max tried not to laugh at the look on Keiko's face. "This is my social media director and co-designer."

Max knew Keiko didn't like being called her assistant, and besides, it was no longer an accurate description of her job.

Keiko, always wary of strangers, reached out for a handshake, no doubt hoping to avoid cheek kisses. Xavier took her hand, but instead of shaking it, turned it over and planted a kiss on the back. Max suppressed a laugh when Keiko snatched her hand back.

As they walked away from Xavier, Keiko muttered, "Well, that's a first. I didn't know people still did that."

"He's a dying breed." Richard led them through the crowd into the main room. Max's attention was captured by the diversity of the gallery's clientele and the variety of fashion displayed by the guests, including a woman in a colorful sari and a tall, thin man in a topcoat and tails.

Keiko walked up to a four-foot-tall abstract painting, and Richard and Max joined her as she stared at it. "It looks like the ocean. Is it supposed to be the ocean?"

Richard grinned. "Yes. Very perceptive of you."

"I like the ones you used to paint. I knew they were the ocean without having to ask."

"I liked them too," Max said. "But I think I like these even better."

"Hopefully, the art-buying public agrees with you," Richard said as Xavier approached.

"You must mingle," he hissed, and pulled Richard into the crowd.

Max and Keiko walked from painting to painting,

noticing most of the guests seemed more interested in socializing and posing for pictures.

Keiko squinted at each canvas, as if she were trying to visualize the waves or the people on the shore.

Andrea returned with champagne-filled flutes for Keiko and Max. They continued to weave their way through the crowd and stepped down into an adjacent room where other artists' works were on display. The crowds were thinner here.

Keiko paused in front of a large painting of a cottage on the top of a cliff glowing from a light within. "Is this one of your dad's?"

"This is one of Leo Baldassari's pieces." Max leaned closer to take a look at the placard next to it. "Holy—" She stopped herself. "I mean, my goodness. I didn't know his paintings were that expensive."

"They weren't." Max turned to see who spoke. It was Eliana. "After his death, the prices of his works more than doubled. Are you enjoying the opening?"

"Keiko and I just got here." Max motioned to where Keiko had just been standing, but Richard now stood in her place. "Hi, Dad. Where'd Keiko go?"

"I think she's making sure everyone gets the right hashtags when they post their pictures." Richard gave Eliana a kiss on the cheek. "I'm so glad you could make it. I hope this isn't too hard on you."

"Thank you, dear. As if losing your husband suddenly wasn't bad enough, Xavier has informed me that with the exception of this one painting, Leo took back his artwork and had made arrangements with another gallery." Eliana stared over Max's shoulder.

Max followed her gaze and saw Xavier talking with a tall, young man wearing a black sweater and slacks. "Where did he take it?" she asked.

Eliana turned back to Max. "I have no idea. I've called every gallery in town."

"But you must have other paintings of his."

"I have a few of his smaller pieces. But never mind that now. This is your father's night. What a wonderful turnout."

"Yes, thanks to Keiko," Richard said.

"Perhaps, but also because of your beautiful paintings." Eliana turned to Max. "It's nice to see you again. Perhaps we'll have more of a chance to chat later." She slipped away into the crowd.

"Was it something I said?" Max asked her father as he watched Eliana walk away. What did that look on his face mean? Concern? Or something more?

"She's just a bit vulnerable right now," Richard said as his eyes followed her. "You remember how I was the first year after I lost your mother."

Max decided to change the subject. This was supposed to be a happy night, after all. "What time is this big announcement?"

"Nine o'clock." Richard glanced at his watch. "That's only ten minutes away—I'd better find Xavier."

Why did Eliana only have a few small pieces of her late husband's art? Richard's house was full of his canvases, hung on the walls or stacked in his studio, but if Richard's artworks commanded as much as that single Baldassari painting, perhaps he would sell every last one.

Max surveyed the room looking for a friendly face. She recognized an older woman with a long silver braid and headed over to greet Teresa McNulty, one of the owners of the Knitpickers yarn store. When she got closer, she saw that she was with her fiancé Simon Abbot.

"Max, I knew you'd be here," Teresa said, giving her a quick hug. "This is so exciting."

"Hello Teresa, hello Simon. Where's Fiona?"

"My sister's here somewhere being a social butterfly, as usual. We came back here to get away from the crowd for a moment."

"It's so nice of you both to come to support my dad. What do you think of his new style?"

"They are stunning, simply stunning," Teresa said. "We're here to provide moral support of course, but Simon is also very interested in acquiring some of Richard's paintings to add to his collection, aren't you, dear?"

"What?" He seemed distracted by a sculpture displayed on a pedestal. "Yes. Very interested."

"You have a sculpture quite like that, don't you, dear?" Teresa said, stepping closer and looking at the placard on the stand. "How odd. Isn't yours a Baldassari? It says the artist is Bennett Landis, but it looks so similar. I've never heard of him, have you?"

"Artists are always copying one another," Simon

said, seeming to brush off her question. "Big night for your father, Max. How is he enjoying the attention? He'd better get used to it, if tonight is any indication."

"I think he's enjoying himself quite a bit."

"Is that him?" Teresa asked. "Surrounded by women?"

Max spun around to see her dad in a circle of four women who were hanging on his every word. "Do you think he needs rescuing?"

Simon laughed. "You're the only one who would think that, but in this case you might be right. I wanted to speak with him anyway. Be right back, darling." He kissed Teresa on the cheek.

As soon as he was out of earshot, Teresa whispered, "That sculpture looks so much like ours, it's hard to believe it isn't the same artist. We found it in a little gallery in La Paz."

"La Paz?" Max asked, trying to remember her geography but failing. "Where is that?"

"It's in South America."

"Bolivia?" Max guessed.

"Yes, that's right. The man at the gallery told us the Baldassaris were living there at the time, although we never saw them. They kept their house here while they traveled all over the world. It seems an extravagance to own a home in Crystal Shores when you spend so little time here, but I suppose they could afford it. It's such an adorable little cottage. You know the one on Hyacinth with the turret?"

"I love that house. It's just one or two houses up from Ocean Drive, right?" Max asked.

"That's the one. I've heard she's put it up for sale."

"And that's not all you've heard, I'm guessing," Max coaxed, hoping for more details about the widow her dad seemed so protective of.

A familiar voice behind her said, "Max, since when did you become interested in gossip?"

Max turned to see Fiona with a sly grin on her face. "Since a certain woman's been hanging around my dad, to be honest."

"Good for you," Fiona said. "Richard is one of the most eligible men in town, and not every woman has good intentions."

Teresa shook her head. "You're so suspicious. Most people are basically good."

"Yes," Fiona agreed. "The operative word is 'most.' That leaves plenty of people who are trouble. So… who are we talking about?"

"Eliana Baldassari," Max said, not trying to hide her misgivings. "My dad seems completely taken in by her."

"Max, that's so unlike you," Teresa said. "Are you sure that's not just you being overprotective?"

Max thought this over for a moment. "I suppose you could be right. It's just that she seems like the type of woman who's used to getting what she wants, and I'm worried that what she wants now is my dad."

"Would that be so terrible?" Teresa asked.

"At least we know she's not after him for his money," Fiona said. "Her late husband's artwork is worth twice as much now that he's dead. She must be set for life."

"Except she says she only has a few pieces. Doesn't that seem odd to you?" Max shushed them when she saw Eliana walk past following Xavier. "Excuse me, ladies."

Max wandered through the crowd, trying to look casual, as she followed Eliana and Xavier to the back of the gallery. They slipped down a narrow hallway and into a room on the left, closing the door behind them. On the right, Max peered into a room full of empty frames leaned up against the walls. She heard voices coming from behind the door that Eliana and Xavier had just entered, so she ducked into the little room, hoping she could hear the conversation from her hiding place. She was in luck. The walls were apparently very thin, and Eliana didn't seem concerned about being overheard.

"You can't keep ignoring me." Max recognized Eliana's voice.

"This is not the time or place," Xavier answered.

"It never is. I want to know what you meant when you said you don't have any of Leo's artwork."

"I only have the one. I'm sure you saw it in the gallery."

"What about his sculptures? You have one on display right now."

"No, no, that's another artist. Didn't you look at the card? You know you can't copyright a style." Xavier sounded defensive. Was he hiding something?

"A month ago, you had at least a dozen of his paintings."

"I told you already. Leo showed up with a van and took everything with him."

"When was that?" Eliana demanded.

"Just before the two of you went to Mexico that last time."

There was a long pause. "You're lying," she hissed.

"I'm telling you, he just turned up one day unannounced and told me he was taking everything right then and there. He said he had another gallery lined up, and he was terminating his contract."

"If that was the case, you'd have him sign a receipt. You wouldn't let him just take it."

"Of course not. Come back next week—"

Eliana practically shouted. "I want to see it now."

"Quiet, my dear," Xavier said. "People will hear."

Eliana lowered her voice. "If I don't get those paintings back, you'll pay. Believe me when I tell you, you don't want to cross me."

CHAPTER 6

*M*ax didn't want to get caught eavesdropping, so she slipped out of her hiding place and strolled nonchalantly back toward the main gallery.

She turned a corner and stopped just in time to avoid running straight into a tall, slender man with dark hair and pale skin. He looked as if he never went out in the sun. "Hey, have you seen my dad?" he asked. She recognized him as the young man Xavier had been talking with earlier.

"That depends. Who's your dad?"

"Xavier Hildalgo."

"Really?"

He shrugged. "Really. At least that's what my mom says."

"I'm Max Walters, Richard Walters' daughter."

"Nice to meet you," he said with a curt nod. "I'm

Henry Hildalgo. I'm going to have a gallery show here soon."

"Oh, really?" Max gave him an encouraging smile. "So, you're an artist, too?"

His demeanor brightened. "I work in objét trouve." He must have seen Max's blank look, because he interpreted the phrase for her. "Found art."

The translation didn't help. "That's interesting," she said, hoping that was an appropriate response. Apparently, it was.

"It is, but only if you have the eye to see beauty and meaning in everyday items. Not everyone has the necessary sensibility, so it's up to artists like me to go out in the world and find objects that have been tossed aside and interpret them for the hoi polloi."

"Tossed aside? Like trash?" The moment the words came out of her mouth, Max hoped she hadn't offended him.

"Yes, exactly." He grinned and reached in his pocket for a card. "Here's my card with my website. You can sign up online to get notified of my next showing."

"Okay," Max said, taking the card from him.

"It's great to meet a fan, but I really must talk to my father." He held up a postcard with the gallery's name on it. "He's made a mistake on the schedule for next month. Have you seen him?"

She pointed to the back of the gallery. "I think he's in his office." She turned and scanned the room for Keiko. She found her talking with Olivia and Zach.

Olivia gave Max a hug. "This is so exciting. What a

turnout!"

"It's really something, isn't it?" Max agreed.

Keiko must have been able to tell that Max had something on her mind. "What's going on?" she asked quietly so the others wouldn't hear. Before Max could answer, she noticed Richard heading their way.

"I'll tell you later," Max whispered.

"Hi, girls," he said cheerfully, his cheeks flushed. "And Zach. Are you having a good time?"

"Not as good as you, by the looks of it," Max said. "No more champagne for you."

Richard laughed. "You're probably right. I think they've run out anyway. Xavier said he sold five of my paintings tonight. Isn't that great?" He leaned closer and added quietly, "That's more than I made all last year."

"That's great Dad. Now, why don't we give you a ride home?"

"I can't leave until the big announcement," Richard insisted. "You'll stay too, won't you?" He looked at her hopefully. "By the way, where is Jason?"

"He's working, as usual." Max said. "He sent his good wishes."

Eliana emerged from the back of the gallery and put on a radiant smile when she saw Richard. "Isn't it time for your big announcement?"

"Yes," Simon said, appearing by his side. "Tonight is a big success for you, Richard. Your life won't be the same from now on out. I came early to get first pick, and I wasn't the only one. I almost came to blows with another collector, but we settled it amicably. I would wager you sold at least ten paintings before the show even opened."

Richard knitted his brow and looked from Simon to Max.

"Aren't you happy, Richard?" Simon asked.

Richard smiled and said, "Yes, of course. Very happy." He turned to Eliana. "Have you seen Xavier?"

"No," she answered. "I haven't seen him since I first arrived. Why?"

Max stared at her, wondering why she had just lied.

"We were supposed to make the announcement fifteen minutes ago," Richard explained. "I'll see if I can find him."

As Richard walked toward the back of the gallery, Max heard someone call her name.

Eric waved over people's heads until he caught Max's eye. "Goodness, what a crowd. That doorman wanted me to wait in line. Can you imagine?"

Max glanced at Keiko, who was trying not to snicker. "No, I can't imagine. I hope you told him how important you were."

"Don't get sassy with me, young lady. I slipped him a twenty. That did it."

"You didn't," Max said.

"Don't look so outraged. You two didn't stand in line, did you?"

"Well, no, but..."

"Nepotism and cold hard cash," Eric explained. "That's how the world works. Let the unfortunate ones without money or well-placed relatives wait their turn."

Max shook her head. Sometimes she wasn't sure she liked the way the world worked, even if it worked in her favor this particular time.

Keiko asked Eric his opinion of abstract art.

"I'd rather see one of those paintings that's all white and looks like a blank canvas than see a Baldassari. That man is a hack."

"Was a hack," Max corrected.

"Did something change?" Eric asked. "Did he acquire some measure of artistic talent recently?"

"No, he died."

"I suppose it's in poor taste to speak ill of the dead," Eric said, "so I'll keep my opinions to myself. He was a marketing genius. I will say that."

They chatted as Max showed Eric around the gallery, planning to show him her favorite paintings, but she found it difficult to be heard in the dense crowd. They returned to the back of the gallery where it was quieter.

"Shush," Eric said. "Do you hear someone calling your name?"

Max turned and saw her father with a wild look on his face. She hurried to his side.

"Call the paramedics. It's Xavier," he said through gritted teeth.

"What do you mean, it's Xavier?" Max asked.

Richard closed his eyes tightly and when he reopened them, said simply, "I think he's dead."

CHAPTER 7

*T*he fear in her father's eyes sent a shiver down Max's spine. Time slowed and Eric's voice sounded far away as he spoke to the dispatcher.

"What do you mean, dead?" Max asked Richard. Of course, she knew what dead meant, but coherent thought seemed to elude her. She'd never known her father to show fear. He was her rock. "Did he have a heart attack? An accident?"

Richard shook his head. "I don't know." Max broke free of his grasp and ran toward the office.

The office door was slightly ajar, and she pushed on it, being careful not to touch the doorknob. She slipped inside, but the dead body she expected to find wasn't there. A marble bust lay on the floor next to an over-sized ebony desk. She took a few steps into the room to look behind the desk and discovered Xavier lying on his chest, his face turned to one side. He looked very dead. Just in case, she forced herself to walk closer to check for a pulse. Judging by the pool of blood forming by his head, there was no point, but she knelt down and felt his wrist just to be sure.

The ascot Xavier wore was disheveled, and Max wondered if he had struggled with his attacker. The color of the silk reminded her of something, but it took her a moment to make the connection. The lavender dress. It was nearly the same color as the gown she'd just ordered for one of her clients.

Xavier must have been hit on the back of the head, and the bust had her vote for the most likely murder weapon. Assuming it was solid marble, it would have done the job with one blow. She took her phone out of her pocket and called Jason.

"Hi, Max. I really can't talk right now. I'm busy."

"Well, you're about to get busier. There's been a murder."

"What do you mean, a murder?" he asked. "Where?"

"At the gallery." She took another look at the motionless body. "It's Xavier Hildalgo, the gallery owner."

"Did you call 9-1-1?"

"Of course," she said with a huff. "I mean I didn't, but Eric did. I'll keep everyone out of the office until you get here."

"It's not my jurisdiction, Max," Jason said.

"What?" Of course. They were in Laguna Beach. Her mind tried to find the right words to say, but all she could think of was, "Sorry to bother you."

"Are you okay? Do you need anything?"

Yes. She needed a hug. She needed her boyfriend to be here by her side, which he would have been if they hadn't had a fight. If he hadn't decided to move all the way across the country.

"No. I'm fine, thanks." She ended the call before he could say anything else or before she said something she might regret later.

She shouldn't be in here. Someone might question what she was doing, but as long as she didn't touch anything, it couldn't hurt to take a quick look, could it? A few papers lay neatly on the desk, along with a framed picture of his son, and a Tiffany style lamp. No obvious signs of a struggle.

She took a step toward the bust. Carved, curly hair topped the classic face with its long nose. A name etched into the base said Hermes.

Besides the desk, the room contained a tall bookshelf, a filing cabinet, and a hat rack. She turned to the bookshelf. An empty space on one of the middle shelves might have held the bust before it had become a weapon. She took a few steps closer to get a better look. Luckily, today must not have been cleaning day, because a thin layer of dust lay undisturbed with a notable absence in one area.

Glancing at the bust and comparing the size of the base to the dust-free impression on the shelf, Max confirmed that the bust must have been sitting in that spot minutes earlier. She took a quick look at the other shelves, not expecting to find any other clues, but on the next higher shelf there was a nearly identical shape in the dust. Had there been two busts?

A quick survey of the room didn't reveal another bust or any other similarly shaped object.

The hat rack was hatless, holding only a man's overcoat, the type more often seen on the east coast. It seemed odd that Xavier had a heavy coat but no hat, until Max reminded herself this was California, not New York, and few men owned overcoats, much less hats.

Max nearly jumped out of her skin when she heard rapping at the door.

"Max," a voice whispered. "It's me."

"Dad?"

She slipped out of the office where her father waited for her. Eric stood nearby, keeping people away from the office door with an air of casual effortlessness, persuading them that there was nothing at all wrong.

What was she going to tell the police when they asked about her father? She knew he had nothing to do with Xavier's death, but would the police come to the same conclusion? Her dad would do anything for her.

"Dad?" she whispered. "Would you lie to protect someone you loved?"

He seemed surprised by her question, and then understanding dawned on his face. "You don't want to know what I would do. You don't need to know. But you're not me. I didn't kill him, and you don't need to lie for me. Jason knows I'd never kill anyone."

"This is not Jason's jurisdiction, unfortunately. Before the police get here, I need to ask you something. Where were you for ten minutes or so before you found Xavier's body?"

Before he could answer, shouts of someone yelling, "Move aside, move aside," interrupted them. The doorman pushed through the crowd followed by two paramedics shouldering red trauma bags. The bouncer pointed them to the office and once they had closed the office door, he sauntered over to Eric. The big tip must have made an impression on him.

"Hey," the bouncer said casually. "What's going on? Someone hurt?"

"You could say so," Eric said noncommittally. "Your boss."

"Not my boss," the man said. "I work for an agency." He turned to go back to the front of the gallery, and the growing crowd parted to make way for him.

Eric resumed crowd control and calmly told anyone who asked that there had been a minor incident. "A possible heart attack, but it might just be heartburn. You never know about these things. It's best to be on the safe side."

He had almost convinced the curious gallery guests that nothing was out of the ordinary when a booming voice called out.

"Laguna Beach Police Department. Make way."

Detective John Gallagher appeared in all his rumpled brown glory, much to Max's dismay.

The feeling was obviously mutual. "Great," he said

in way of greeting. "I thought I was done with you when I transferred to Laguna Beach."

"Nice to see you too, Detective," Max said, in an attempt to be polite even if he wasn't giving her the same courtesy.

His size and lumbering gait reminded her of a bear, but his face was more like a bloodhound with several chins that rolled over his collar and a mouth permanently turned down at the corners.

"Hi, Randy," she said to the uniformed officer behind Gallagher. He'd been a classmate of hers through middle and high school.

"That's Officer Rivera to you," Gallagher barked. "Who found the victim?"

"My father did," Max said. She turned around, expecting to find Richard behind her, but she didn't see him among the onlookers. She turned back to the detective. "Richard Walters. He checked his pulse and asked us to call for help."

"We'll need to question both of you. Don't leave," he ordered.

"What about—?" Max began to ask.

"We'll take it from here, ma'am," Officer Rivera said as he opened the office door and followed Gallagher inside.

Did Randy just call her ma'am?

She began to replay the evening in her mind, especially the last half hour or so. Why had her dad waited so long between going back to the office and telling them that Xavier was dead? Max hoped he had a good explanation to give to the police. She wasn't going to volunteer the information until she had his side of the story, but she didn't want to lie to the police.

Max walked through the thinning crowd searching for Richard. A number of gallery patrons clustered by the front door. As soon as Keiko spotted her, she rushed over to ask Max what had happened, but so did ten other people, none of whom was her father.

"I need some fresh air," she said, motioning Keiko to follow her outside.

When they reached the front door, a long line of people waited to exit. Two uniformed officers were speaking to each person before they were permitted to leave.

"What is the holdup?" Keiko asked.

"They're probably deciding who they want to question tonight and getting names and contact information for everyone else. Most of them don't know anything anyway."

Keiko saw Fiona further up the line and went to confirm Max's theory while Max waited. Richard appeared by her side and touched her elbow. "Come with me."

Richard led her to the back of the gallery past the office door. It was slightly open, and Max could see Gallagher's back and assumed that Randy was in there with him. Luckily, neither of them saw her or her father passing by in the hall.

The rear wall had a loading area with a big aluminum roll up door and a small door next to it. Two uniformed officers guarding the rear exit stopped talking to each other and addressed them.

"You'll need to exit through the front," one of the officers said.

"We're waiting to be questioned by Detective Gallagher," Richard said. This seemed to satisfy them, and they returned to their conversation.

Before Max could ask what Richard was up to, he took her arm and they slipped into an alcove out of sight of the officers and ducked behind a tall cabinet. They were standing in a short passageway with a small door at the other end. Did the police know about this exit? No one else, including her, seemed to have noticed it.

Stepping outside into the cool night, they found themselves behind the gallery next to a green dumpster in a gravel parking lot with room for three cars. Four, if they didn't mind getting door dings. Scrubby hedges surrounded the lot, hiding it from the alley behind. A dusty old Porsche that might be black under all the dust leaned to one side. It had a flat tire.

"How did you know about this exit?" Max asked.

"I didn't. Not until I went to talk to Xavier. I saw someone slip out of the office carrying a duffle bag and run this way. I thought it was odd, so I followed him."

"But he might have been the murderer. You might be the only person who can identify him."

"I didn't get much of a look at him. He went through the hedges there." He pointed at a gap in the shrubbery. "I followed, but when I came out the other side, I'd lost him. I looked for a while before I gave up. That's when I came back and found Xavier."

"Did anyone see you?" Max couldn't help but think her father might need an alibi.

He shook his head slowly, and she wondered if the same thought had occurred to him.

"Can you describe him?"

"I didn't get a close look at him." Richard said. "The hallway was dark, and I only caught a glimpse of him before he slipped out the back door."

"Let me guess. Medium height, medium build, brown hair…"

He shrugged. "Around my height, I think. But I'm just guessing. I only got a quick look at him."

That might be helpful. Her dad was six feet tall. "What about his hair? Dark, light, curly?"

"No idea. He was wearing a black fedora."

"He might have been the murderer, you know." A thought occurred to her. "Are you sure it was a man?"

Richard paused to think. "I think it was a man." He sighed. "But I suppose it could have been a tall woman. Well, I'll tell the police, and they'll make what they can out of it."

"Come on," Max said. "Let's join the others."

"Drat." Richard inspected the sleeve of his sweater. "I've snagged my best cashmere pullover."

"I think the sweater is the least of your problems, Dad."

If Jason had been investigating, she wouldn't have this sinking feeling in her stomach. With Detective Gallagher on the case, her father might be in for a long night of questioning.

CHAPTER 8

*D*etective Gallagher finally emerged from the office and lumbered over to them with Randy following close behind and carrying two folding chairs. He stepped up to Richard. "Please accompany Officer Rivera," he said, motioning to the storage room where Max had stood when she eavesdropped on Xavier and Eliana. She watched her father follow Randy and his folding chairs into the little room.

"Follow me," Gallagher said, and stepped into a small room next to the office. As she stepped inside, she smelled varnish or paint thinner. A worktable took up most of the room, and she guessed this was where they built and finished picture frames.

Gallagher sat behind the worktable, and Max sat down in the only other chair facing him across the table.

"May I see your identification?" he asked, though it sounded more like an order than a request.

"You know who I am, Detective," she said.

"Your identification," he repeated.

She pulled her driver's license out of her phone case and handed it to him. "Was the cause of death blunt force trauma?"

He said nothing as he copied her information into his notebook. When he handed her license back, he said, "Before I tell you any information, I need to establish where you were at the time of the murder."

"What time was that?" she asked. "Have you established time of death?"

Gallagher didn't look up from his notebook, but his neck reddened, which couldn't be a good sign. "Why don't you start by telling me where you were when your father discovered the body?"

Max answered his questions, providing as much detail as she could recall. When he stood as if ready to conclude the interview, she held up a hand.

"One more thing," she said. "I heard Xavier and Eliana arguing earlier. Around nine o'clock, I think."

He clenched his jaw tightly but said nothing until he was seated again. "And you didn't mention it, because?"

"I just did,' Max said, trying not to sound defensive. "I answered all of your questions honestly and thoroughly, but you didn't ask me if I knew anything else that was relevant." She knew she was implying that he wasn't doing his job very well, but she wasn't going to let him act like she wasn't being cooperative.

He took a deep breath, as if trying to control his temper. "Do you remember what was said?"

Max repeated the argument as well as she could remember it, not leaving out a single detail, except for the fact that she was hiding in a storage room at the time.

After she finished, Gallagher asked, "And is there anything else you would like to mention before we conclude this interview?"

"No," Max said. "If I think of anything else, I'll call you."

"Goodie." He made no attempt to hide his sarcasm. "Please do."

Randy hadn't completed his interview with Richard, but Gallagher wouldn't allow her to wait for him inside the gallery. When she stepped outside, she found herself alone in the chilly night air. She wished she'd brought her jacket.

"Want a ride?"

Max turned around to see Keiko sitting on the edge of a planter. "I didn't see you there."

Keiko stood and tried to brush the wrinkles out of her skirt. "My car is right around the corner."

On the drive home, Max told Keiko about the argument she'd overheard between Xavier and Eliana."

"Wow," Keiko said. "Did you tell Detective Gallagher?"

"Yes. It was hard to tell what he thought about it. He's so rude to me, and he wouldn't share any information, not even time of death."

"I think we can narrow that down as well as he can," Keiko said.

"You're probably right."

"And he's only rude because you're a better detective than he is." Keiko pulled her sedan in front of Max's house. "Plus, you have people skills, which he has no clue about."

Max said goodnight and walked around the back of her father's house. But instead of climbing the stairs to her apartment, she decided to wait in Richard's living room for him. It was well after one in the morning when he finally came home.

"I'm going to bed, Max," he told her with a tired voice. "I'm beat."

"I'm sure you are. But what happened with the interview? Is Gallagher considering you a suspect?"

"No," Richard said. "I told Officer Rivera about the person I saw, so after he finished with me, Gallagher asked me some more questions. His theory, as far as I can tell, is that Xavier surprised a thief in his office and that's who I saw leaving out the back door."

Max felt the relief rush over her. She hadn't realized how worried she'd been until that moment. She gave her father a hug and said goodnight.

When she finally crawled into bed, she lay awake thinking. How could Xavier have surprised a burglar when he was already in the office? Perhaps he'd left the office after talking to Eliana and gone back in. Max couldn't shut off her mind. The events of the evening replayed in her mind while she listened to the night noises and watched the moon cast eerie shadows in her room.

CHAPTER 9

*M*ax slept through her alarm and woke in a panic when a bright sunbeam fell across her face. Seeing the time, she hurried to get ready and set off in a brisk walk to Wedding Belles.

Once inside the shop, after putting a pot of coffee on to brew, she plopped into the closest overstuffed easy chair, sunk back into the down cushions, and closed her eyes.

The shop phone rang, and she let it go to voice mail, unwilling to leave the cozy comfort of her chair. Eric was so right when he suggested down fill. It was so soft. She closed her eyes and was nearly asleep when a tapping sound made her jump.

A face peering through the door between the blinds startled her wide awake. When she recognized Keiko's dark eyes, she waved her in, realizing that her protégé was the one person she wanted to see this morning.

Instead of entering, Keiko made a motioning

gesture with her head and mouthed something. Max reluctantly pushed herself up out of the chair and walked to the door.

"It's not locked," Max began as she opened the door but stepped aside when she saw Keiko had her hands full. Two large cups of what she hoped was a caffeinated beverage, and a bag from Rose Cafe. "You're a lifesaver. How did you know I would be in serious need of coffee?"

"I see all and know all," she said with a little shrug, and headed for the workroom that often doubled as a lunchroom.

Max followed her, smiling in spite of herself and hoping the bag contained something chocolate. Right now, she'd settle for a gluten-free fat-free muffin. Keiko covered the worktable with an oilskin tablecloth she'd made for the purpose and tore open the bag to reveal croissants. Not just any croissants. Chocolate croissants. And they were still warm.

Keiko let her boss eat her pastry in silence, but Max knew she must have a million questions.

Max ate the last bite of melty chocolaty goodness, took a big sip of her cappuccino, and leaned back in her chair. "Okay, shoot."

Keiko blinked innocently. "I am not here for gossip."

Max laughed. "No, that will be Fiona later. She showed remarkable restraint by not ambushing me as soon as I arrived. But you must be curious."

Keiko's eyes widened. "Are you planning to investigate?"

"No." She laughed. "I don't have time to investigate a murder. But I'm curious too."

"You really will stay out of it this time?" Keiko didn't appear the least bit convinced.

"Yes. I just want to go over what we know, so I'm prepared if the police need to question me again. Or I might remember something that's relevant."

"Okay," Keiko said. "Why don't you tell me what you remember?"

"I was worried last night because my dad went to talk to Xavier at least ten minutes before he actually found the body. He followed someone wearing a fedora and carrying a duffle bag out the back door, but he doesn't have much of a description. Did you see anyone wearing a fedora last night?"

"No," Keiko said. "I think I would have noticed."

"Me neither. The problem is, my dad doesn't have an alibi."

"Why would he need one?"

Max hesitated. "I know he didn't kill Xavier. My dad doesn't like killing spiders. He carries them out to the garden."

"What are you not telling me?" Keiko asked.

"I don't know. There's just something that doesn't add up. When he told me not to lie for him, he said something that made me think he would lie for someone else. Someone he loved."

Keiko gasped. "He's covering for you?"

"What? No, of course not."

"Okay then, who?"

"Eliana."

Keiko cocked her head to one side. "He's in love with Eliana? When did that happen? I didn't even realize they were dating. Are they dating?"

"He says they're not, but I don't know if I believe him. He's completely taken in by her. What if he's been in love with her for a while? What if she's in some sort of trouble, and she killed Xavier? What if Xavier attacked her in that office, and she grabbed the statue and …"

"Slow down," Keiko cautioned. "Where is this coming from? Just because Eliana was upset with Xavier doesn't mean she killed him. Maybe your feelings about her are clouding your judgment."

"What do you mean my feelings? I don't even know her."

"No," Keiko said, "But, I know you. And you can't forget what she said at the restaurant the first time you saw her, can you? She might have been joking or being sarcastic or something like that."

"Maybe." Max wasn't sure if she agreed with Keiko.

"And maybe you are being protective of your father," Keiko said. "You have good instincts about people, but you could be wrong just this once."

Max gave Keiko a sheepish grin. "As unlikely as that is, I suppose it's a possibility. But I don't trust her. Especially after hearing her threaten Xavier."

"I understand, but that does not make her a murderer. How heavy was that statue anyway?"

Max paused. "I don't know. It was a marble bust of Hermes about a foot tall. Marble is heavy, isn't it?"

"Very heavy," Keiko agreed. "There was a statue of Hermès the designer?" She stood up, threw her trash away, and headed for the office.

Max followed her. "Hermes was a Greek god, I think. Are you going to look it up?"

Keiko sat down in front of the computer. "I don't really care about some Greek god, but I am going to look up how heavy a marble bust is."

Ten minutes later, Keiko informed Max that a piece of marble that size would likely weigh eighty to ninety pounds.

"No way could Eliana pick up something that heavy," Max said.

Keiko nodded. "It seems unlikely. It would be hard enough for a strong man to lift it. I would say that settles it. In spite of your feelings toward Eliana, it appears she is not a murderer."

"No, but I have some other names to call her."

"Max!" Keiko objected.

Max grinned. "I'll just keep them to myself."

Max sequestered herself in the sewing room hoping to catch up on her projects now that she was the only seamstress available. Just before lunchtime, she heard the door jingle and peeked into the showroom in time to see Eric placing a large bouquet on the coffee table.

"I thought you might need some cheering up."

"Why is that?" Max asked.

Eric rearranged a few blooms, as if the arrangement

wasn't perfect already. "That horrible detective kept Richard at the gallery for hours questioning him. You must be terribly worried."

"No, I'm not worried," Max insisted. "My father didn't kill Xavier."

"Well, of course he didn't," Eric agreed.

"Did you see someone wearing a fedora last night at the gallery?" Max asked.

"Let me think," Eric shook his head. "No, there was one man in a top hat, one with a turban, and another in a tasteless red ball cap. No fedoras. Why?"

"My dad saw someone in a fedora go out the back exit just before he discovered Xavier's body. The police think he's the murderer. And as soon as they find the guy, case closed."

Eric grinned. "I'm so relieved to hear you say that. I'll just take the flowers back, then." He reached for the vase.

"No, you don't," Max protested.

"Just kidding. I can write off the expense on my taxes, anyway." He artfully fanned out a stack of fliers for his flower shop next to the bouquet. "Now, how about I take you to lunch?"

Max hesitated. "I don't think I can spare the time."

"You have turned me down every time I've tried to make plans with you for the past month. I won't take no for an answer."

Keiko called out from the office, "Go to lunch. Heidi will be here shortly, and I can watch the shop myself until she gets here."

"There," Eric said. "It's settled. My car is right out front."

Max climbed into the passenger side of his BMW. "So where are we going?" She knew that Eric only frequented the best restaurants. She hoped for an ocean view, but when he turned off Coast Highway, he headed east instead of west.

Max eyed him as he turned into a parking lot. "Roger's Gardens? I thought you were taking me to lunch. Are we going to munch on begonias and oleander?"

"Hardly," Eric said with a dramatic sigh. "Oleander is poisonous. Haven't you heard about the new restaurant at the Gardens?"

Max squealed. "You're taking me to the Farmhouse?"

"I am," Eric said with a satisfied smile.

"I hope you made a reservation," Max said. "I've heard it's almost impossible to get a table there, even at lunch time." She stopped when she saw the look on Eric's face.

"How long have you had these memory issues?" he asked.

"Memory issues?" Max had no idea what he meant.

"Yes, apparently you've forgotten who you're with. Of course, I have a reservation, not that I need one. But restaurant owners do appreciate it when you call ahead."

"Sorry," Max said. "You're right. I thought I was talking to a mere mortal. What was I thinking?"

Eric pulled his car into a spot. "Just don't let it happen again."

The Farmhouse at Roger's Gardens was an outdoor restaurant in the middle of a nursery that was the Disneyland of nurseries.

They walked up to the hostess who greeted Eric by name. She sat them at one of the best tables at the far end of the restaurant overlooking opulent greenery and a surprising number of blooming plants, considering it was December.

The server appeared out of nowhere and filled their water glasses, leaving a crystal carafe on the table. "A glass of pinot for you?" he asked Eric.

Eric nodded, and the waiter turned to Max.

"I'll have an iced tea, please." She didn't want to be tipsy and trying to assist clients, although some days she thought it might help.

After the waiter left, Max whispered to Eric, "Boy, you know this is a fancy restaurant when they give you water without having to ask for it." California seemed to be in perpetual drought.

"Stick with me, kid, and you might even get a straw for your drink," Eric replied.

When the server returned with Eric's wine and Max's iced tea, her mouth began to water listening to the server describe the specials. She opted for curry and coconut crusted Icelandic cod and Eric ordered a citrus glazed salmon salad.

"So how is the investigation going?" Eric asked as he sipped his wine.

"I'm not investigating."

Eric narrowed his eyes. "That doesn't sound like you at all."

"I'm extremely busy with the shop and I'm behind schedule on my special orders," Max said. "I'm sure the police will find out whoever killed Xavier."

"You mean Detective Gallagher?" he asked.

The server reappeared with their entrees. Max picked up her fork to take a bite of the delicious looking dish. It was heavenly.

Eric waited for her to finish several bites before he resumed his questioning. "All of a sudden you have complete confidence in Detective Gallagher's investigative skills? When did that happen?"

"He's trained and experienced."

"Uh, huh," Eric said.

"Look," Max said, feeling her frustration rise. "I'm behind on my sewing, I have orders to place, and I'm still training Heidi. Plus, my boyfriend is moving to Miami."

"What?" Eric said. "When were you planning to tell me this?"

"I just did," Max put down her fork. She didn't feel like eating anymore. "He asked me to go with him."

"He did propose!" Eric seemed pleased by his conclusion. He must have seen the look on her face. "And you said no?"

"No," she corrected him. "He didn't propose."

"Honey, I'm so sorry." Eric placed a hand over his heart. "This is the first time I've seen you really in love. It breaks my heart that it's ending this way."

Max thought about what he said. "I don't know if it's ending, but I don't know how it can go on. Do long distance relationships ever work?"

Eric called over the server. "What is the most decadent dessert you have? Preferably very chocolate."

Shortly, a slice of molten chocolate cake covered in fresh whipped cream appeared in front of her.

Eric waited until she finished it before he spoke. "Feel better?"

She leaned back in her chair and let herself take a deep breath. "It was delicious. But what really helps is spending time with my best friend. I really, really needed this. Thank you."

After lunch, they strolled around the gardens. Nearly every worker and some of the customers said hello to him, which wasn't surprising considering he'd been a successful florist in town for over a decade.

The nursery had an area set aside for Christmas plants and decorations. Eric picked out the perfect rosemary plant shaped like a miniature Christmas tree for his mother.

"Should I get some poinsettias for the shop?" Max asked.

"You do, and I'll disown you," Eric said. He led her to a display of white amaryllis, picked out two, and handed them to her. "An early Christmas present," he said. "And a bribe to keep you from buying any poinsettias."

Max liked poinsettias, but she also loved the beautiful amaryllis she was holding in her arms, so she kept her opinion to herself.

"Ready to go back?" he asked as he paid for the plants.

"No," Max said. "But I'd better."

CHAPTER 10

*M*ax had just put her purse away in the office when she heard the sound of the front door opening.

Heidi called out from upstairs, "I'll be right there."

Max found an older, distinguished-looking man standing in the showroom. Max was instantly curious what this grandfatherly-looking man was doing in her bridal shop.

Heidi came half-way down the stairs. "You're back."

"Yes, thank you, Heidi," Max said. "I've got it." She turned to the visitor. "May I help you?"

"My name is Garrett Moore. I'm looking for Max Walters. Is he in?"

Max suppressed a snicker. It wasn't the first time someone had come looking for a man named Max and found her instead. "I'm Max Walters. It's nice to meet you Mr. Moore." She reached out her hand to shake his.

If he was surprised to find that Max was a woman, he didn't show it. He also didn't show any embarrassment for his mistake. "Please call me Garrett." He shook her hand firmly.

"Okay, Garrett. Now that we have all that out of the way, how may I help you?"

"I'm here to apply for the position."

"Position?" The only position she had advertised was for a seamstress to help her with her custom-made gowns. "I don't really have any positions open. Well, except..."

"The seamstress position," he said, finishing her sentence. He grinned and added, "Though in my case, perhaps we'd call the position a seamster?"

"Oh." This was unexpected.

"It seems that quite a few things aren't what they first appear to be, wouldn't you agree, Max?"

"Very true," she admitted. "Um, do you have a resume?"

"I don't think a resume would be helpful in this situation," he said.

"Relevant experience?" she asked.

"I would say, relevant skills rather than experience." He smiled confidently. "Do you have a sewing machine on the premises?"

"Well, of course," Max said.

"May I see it?"

Max didn't see what harm it would do to show this nice older man her setup, so she led him to the back of the shop and into the large workroom where two sewing machines were set up along with a worktable big enough to cut fabric and cabinets full of notions and tools of the trade.

"My," Garrett said appreciatively. "This is a sweet setup."

Max smiled proudly. "Thank you. It saves so much time having everything you need at hand."

"And the right tool for the job as well. I expect you don't have grandchildren running off with your best scissors to cut heaven knows what."

Max laughed. "I've never had that issue, to be honest."

"It's one of the few downsides of having grandchildren, but it can be a problem." He surveyed the room with obvious interest. "Would you happen to have a few spare scraps of fabric?"

Max wasn't sure what he was getting at, but she pulled out her basket of cabbage, and placed it on the worktable before him.

"Yes, of course," he said. "What seamstress is without her cabbage? Would you pick out a few pieces that you don't mind me using?"

"Are you planning to sew something? Right now?"

"If you don't mind." He walked up to one of the sewing machines. "A Bernina 720. Very nice indeed." He took a closer look at the small screen used to program stitches. "Perhaps I should start with your Singer and get to know the Bernina better in the future." He sat down in front of the Singer. "There, I think that will do for now."

Max picked out several pieces of fabric and handed them to him. Then, as an afterthought, she picked out a small piece of ivory silk. She remembered it had been a bear to work with, slipping all over the place. "There are scissors here," she pointed to a tray on the worktable.

Garrett confirmed that the needle was threaded and checked the Singer's settings. "An hour should be more than enough time," he said. "I'm sure you're busy. Don't let me keep you from your work."

Was he throwing her out of her own workroom? "Anything else you need?" she asked.

"I'm sure I'll be just fine," he said, looking at her expectantly as if waiting for her to leave.

She closed the door behind her and chuckled.

"What's so funny?" Keiko asked, emerging from the office.

"Hi," Max said. "I didn't realize you were here."

"I just got back two minutes ago. I found out some interesting information for you."

"That's nice," Max said, her mind still on Garrett. "Do you know what you call a male seamstress?"

"Is this a riddle?" Keiko asked. "I was never any good at riddles."

"Nope, it's a real question about a real male seamstress." She looked at the clock. "We'll find out in an hour if we need to know what to call him or not, but I have a feeling our next seamster is in the work room."

"What's his name?" Keiko asked.

"Garrett Moore."

Keiko's eyebrows shot up. "Are you kidding me? *The* Garrett Moore?"

Max was confused. "Why would I kid you about hiring a seamster?"

"Not that," Keiko said. "Garrett Moore designed for Armani for a decade or two before he partnered with Toshikazu Kubo."

"Now I know what you're talking about," Max said, relieved to finally be on the same page. "They're behind Kubomo, right? No wonder you recognized his name." Kubomo had erupted onto the fashion scene several years earlier, and Keiko obsessively followed everything they did, from their fashion shows to their retailing and marketing strategies.

Keiko walked to the back of the shop and opened the workroom door slightly. "Hello," she said. "Sorry to disturb you," and closed the door.

"It's him," Keiko said in her loudest whisper. "The last I heard he was in New York. How did he end up in our workroom?"

Max shrugged. "I guess we'll find out more later. In the meantime, what's this information you're talking about?"

"Right," Keiko said, as if she'd forgotten why she'd stopped by. "Have you ever wondered why no one had mentioned the security cameras?"

"That's right," Max said, brightening. "The security

cameras must show who went into Xavier's office. That's fantastic."

"Slow down," Keiko interrupted. "I just found out there is no camera pointing at Xavier's door."

"Who told you that?" Max asked, again in awe of Keiko's research abilities.

"Never mind," Keiko said. "It is better if I not tell you."

Max opened her mouth to argue but thought better of it. Keiko rarely revealed her sources. "What about the rest of the back area? There must be cameras pointing down the hall. What if there was a break in?"

Keiko shook her head. "There's one camera pointing at the loading area—that big roll up door and the smaller door next to it."

Max threw up her arms in frustration. "Are you kidding me?"

"Think about it." Keiko said. "The security cameras are there to prevent theft. Anything large would have to go out through the loading dock. I don't think anyone else was supposed to know about the second door. You said it was pretty hidden."

"It was completely hidden. I wonder why."

"The gallery was originally half the size it is now. When they expanded, they took over the space next door, and so they had a second rear exit." Keiko headed for the office. "Let me know when Mr. Moore is done sewing. I want to meet him."

Garrett emerged from the workroom before his

hour was up. In his hand, he held a tiny ivory silk gown with lace peeking flirtatiously out from under the hem.

Max took the little dress from him and turned it over and inside out. The set-in sleeves, which Max always found the most difficult to attach, didn't have a single pucker. The workmanship was exceptional, down to a row of tiny seed pearls used as buttons.

"Do you often make doll dresses, Garrett?" Max wondered.

He chuckled. "My granddaughter has quite a collection, though she doesn't play with them anymore. She's started scouring thrift shop for old dolls. She repaints the features, gives them new hair, I make the outfits, and she sells them."

"What an entrepreneurial girl," Max said. "How much does she sell them for?"

"The latest sold for over a hundred dollars. She donates her profits to various causes, and now she's decided to start her own charity to provide art supplies for schools." Garrett smiled, obviously proud of his granddaughter. "She feels, and I agree, that the arts are not given the importance in our society that they should be."

"She sounds like a remarkable young lady," Max said.

Garrett looked hopefully at the doll's dress in Max's hand. "I don't suppose you would let me take that one home to her."

"Of course," Max said, handing him back the dress. "In fact, you're welcome to the rest of my cabbage if you'd like to make more dresses for your grand-daughter and her charity."

"I couldn't take your beautiful fabrics," Garrett said. "Some of those silks are very expensive. Believe me, I know."

"And they're sitting here gathering dust and taking up space. I'd love it if you could put them to good use."

"Thank you for your generous offer," Garrett said. "I accept. Now, about the position."

Max didn't see any reason to think twice. "You're hired," she said, just as Keiko emerged from the office.

"Wonderful," Garrett said. "I can start Monday, if you like."

"Wait," Keiko interrupted. "I'm sorry, but we can't afford you."

"Hello," Garrett said. "I'm—"

"I know who you are," Keiko said. "It's a very great honor to meet you. What I would like to know is why you are applying for a job as a seamstress."

"Seamster," Max corrected.

Garrett regarded Keiko with curiosity. "And you are?"

"Forgive me," Keiko said with a little head bow. "My name is Keiko Hamasaki. I am the website developer and social media director for Wedding Belles Bridal Shop and a consultant for several businesses in town."

"Very nice to meet you, Keiko Hamasaki. I have never before met someone who told me what an honor it was to meet me and then without taking a breath immediately challenged me."

Keiko lowered her head. "My apologies, Mr. Moore."

Garrett roared with laughter. "No need to apologize. No need at all. I could have used you when I was running Kubomo. No matter how hard one tries to avoid it, a leader always ends up surrounded by yes men. Max, you are very lucky to have Keiko Hamasaki in your organization."

Max had never heard her little business referred to as an organization. "I am very aware of how lucky I am." She glanced at Keiko, whose face was beginning to flush with embarrassment. "Keiko does make a good point. The pay I can offer isn't exactly what I'm sure you're used to."

"Your usual rate will do just fine, if we can agree on the other terms."

"Other terms?" Max asked warily.

"I would like to work five days a week starting at nine a.m.—"

"We don't open until ten," Max interrupted.

Garrett nodded. "I will be available for two to four hours per day depending on your needs and my granddaughter's schedule. I may on occasion need time off for trips and such, but I will always give you plenty of notice. Is that satisfactory to you?"

This time, Max waited to see if Keiko had any objections before she spoke. When Keiko had no comment other than a shrug, she said, "That is very satisfactory to me. Keiko, would you be so kind as to assist with the necessary paperwork?"

"Yes, but only after Mr. Moore answers my question."

"Please call me Garrett. What is your question?"

"Why?"

"Ah yes," he said. "I have a strict rule that when someone asks me a question twice, they deserve an answer. When I retired, my wife and I moved here to be close to our grandchildren. I was very surprised to learn that I didn't miss my fast-paced former life. The one thing I did miss was having a place where I was expected to be every day. When I saw your ad for a seamstress, I thought it would be perfect. I find sewing so relaxing, don't you?"

Max shook her head. "Not really," she admitted. "I love designing gowns, but the sewing is my least favorite part."

"Perhaps it's the memories of my grandmother teaching me to sew when I was just a boy in Harlem. My mother was a jazz singer back in those days, and my granny made her beautiful gowns to perform in. All the other singers and even some of the fans started coming to her for gowns. She even made a few for Billie Holliday. Of course, that was when I was just a baby."

"That's fascinating. I'd love to hear more," Max said.

"Listen to this old man telling stories. No wonder my wife wants me out of the house. You young people probably don't know who Billie Holliday was."

"Of course," Keiko said. "Everybody knows him."

"Her," Max corrected. "That's okay. It was a long

time ago. So that's when you became interested in fashion?"

"Yes, and my grandmother saved up to send me to FIT. That's the Fashion Institute of Technology in New York."

"That I knew," Keiko said. "I want to hear about how you started Kubomo. Why did you retire?"

"I'm still a co-owner and advisor, Keiko. I have some great stories to tell you about Toshi one of these days. He's quite a character besides being an exception- ally talented designer." He glanced at his watch. "But I've taken up enough of your time for now. I'll see you Monday morning?"

"I'm looking forward to it," Max said. "Tell you what. I'll come in at nine and show you how the machines work and get you all set up."

"Very well. I look forward to seeing you then."

After Garrett left, Keiko said, "Can you believe it? Garrett Moore is working in your shop. I can't wait to get his advice. I bet he'll have some great suggestions for my clothing line. It's very niche right now, but I've been thinking of growing it into a real business."

"And here I was just happy to have someone to help with the sewing," Max said. "I'm sure he's a wealth of knowledge, but my first priority is going to be catching up on the custom gowns, so I don't have to work so many hours."

"Don't waste this opportunity," Keiko said, before she went into the office and closed the door.

"She's starting to sound like River, with her cryptic

comments," Max muttered to herself. River was their mailman, who always had a wise word or quote for Max. Come to think of it, she hadn't seen him for a week or two. She wouldn't mind hearing some of his sage advice right about now.

CHAPTER 11

*A*fter Garrett left, their next appointment arrived. As Max and Heidi were helping the bride pick out and try on dresses, the phone rang, and Max saw her father's name on the display. She excused herself and stepped into the other room for privacy.

"Dad, what's up? I'm with a client."

"I just came back from another interview with Gallagher," he explained, "although it felt more like an interrogation. I don't think it went well."

"What do you mean?" she asked. "I know he can be kind of a jerk sometimes."

"I'm starting to think he believes I killed Xavier."

"What?" Max didn't know what else to say. "Tell me exactly what he said."

"He said a witness has come forward who saw me go into the office."

"Yes, everyone knows that," Max said. "You found the body."

"No, someone said I went into the office earlier when I followed the burglar out the back. They say I was in there for maybe ten or fifteen minutes before I came back out, but I wasn't in the office more than a minute or two. I explained that to Gallagher, but he seemed think I was lying."

Max tried to make sense of what he was saying. "Who says they saw you?"

"He wouldn't tell me," Richard said. "I know you're busy. I'll talk to you tonight at home. I'm having dinner with a friend, but I shouldn't be out late."

"Wait--" Max protested, but he'd already hung up.

Max floated through the rest of the afternoon in a daze, with Heidi following her around pulling gowns and hanging them back up while they helped a steady stream of brides.

Max's phone rang again just before closing time. She saw Jason's name on the display and let the call go to voicemail.

After Heidi left for the day, Max ran the vacuum over the carpet. She didn't hear the door open over the noise, and she jumped when Jason touched her shoulder.

"Sorry, Max," Jason said, looking sheepish. "I didn't mean to startle you."

She turned off the vacuum and took a few deep breaths waiting for her heartbeat to slow down. "What are you doing here?"

"You wouldn't answer my calls," he explained.

"I've been busy." She wound the cord around the

vacuum and rolled it into the closet where she retrieved the feather duster. She carefully dusted the glass shelves, even though she knew Heidi had already done so earlier that day.

"We need to talk," he said, softly. "About us."

"Please, not now." She put the feather duster down and turned to face him. She saw the concern on his face, but she had other things to worry about at this moment. "My dad was questioned again today, and it doesn't look good. Gallagher told him another witness had come forward." There was little Jason could do, in spite of being a police detective, but maybe there was one question he could answer. "Do you think they'll arrest him?"

"Who is this witness?" Jason asked, "and what did they say?"

Max filled him in on her conversation with her father. "Why would someone lie like that and make my father look guilty?"

"You're sure they're lying?"

Max stiffened. "What are you saying? That my father lied?"

"Don't look at me like that, please." Jason took her hand and gave it a gentle squeeze. "If your father ever lied, he would have a good reason."

Max took a few deep breaths. Would he lie to protect Eliana? "No, there must be another explanation. Maybe someone is out to get my dad, but I can't imagine who." She felt tears welling up but blinked them away. This was no time to fall apart.

"I'll do whatever I can to help," Jason said.

"But there's not much you can do, is there?" She couldn't hold back the tears any longer, and she wiped them away with the back of her hand, not caring if she smeared her makeup.

Jason took her in his arms and held her tightly. "Richard is not going to jail if I can help it."

###

MAX STEPPED INTO THE WORKROOM AND GLANCED AT her to-do list pinned on the bulletin board. She had intended to work on the custom gowns this evening, since one of the clients had a first fitting in less than a week, and Max wasn't even close to being ready. But she couldn't concentrate. So, instead of sewing, she rolled out a yard of white pattern paper onto the worktable and sketched a rough floor plan of the gallery.

Keiko appeared at the doorway. "What are you doing? I thought you went home."

"That's funny. I thought *you* went home."

Keiko shrugged. "Time flies when you start to research your new seamster and learn everything you can to impress him the next time you see him. What about you?"

"I should be sewing, but I wanted to write some things down while they were still fresh in my mind."

Keiko walked closer and looked at her sketch. "Is that the gallery?"

"Yes. I'm writing down where people were the night of the murder," Max said. "I told Gallagher everything I could think of when he questioned me, but maybe I missed something."

"You need a timeline, too," Keiko said. "Starting from when you heard Eliana and Xavier arguing." She found an empty area on the paper and with a ruler and colored pencils, drew a long line with hatches for minutes. She marked the top with a large blue 8:00, and, in green, she marked each five minutes until ten o'clock. "How does that look?"

"Very nice," Max commented on Keiko's artwork. "Eliana was talking with my dad and me around ten minutes till nine, I think. I remember my dad saying they were supposed to make some big announcement at nine." She stopped and turned to Keiko. "I completely forgot about that. What was the announcement, anyway?"

"I think you should ask your dad," Keiko said. "He'll want to be the one to tell you."

"Fine," Max grumbled, returning her attention to their papers. She wrote Eliana's name on the timeline. "I'm guessing it was a little after nine when I followed Eliana and saw her go into Xavier's office. I only listened for a few minutes, and then I ran into Xavier's son, Henry. He asked if I'd seen his dad."

"Okay," Keiko said. "This is only an estimate, but we will say five after nine for the argument, and about five minutes later when you spoke to Henry." She wrote Henry's name down on the timeline. "Did you see Henry go into the office?"

"No, but he headed that way. I wish I had paid more attention." She had no idea at the time that Henry's movements might prove to be important. "And after Eliana reappeared, I remember my dad saying the announcement was fifteen minutes late."

Keiko wrote Eliana's name on the timeline a second time next to 9:15.

"Do you know what time Eric called the paramedics?" Keiko asked.

"Yes. I texted him and asked him to check his phone. It was at exactly nine thirty-one, so when my father said he was going to talk to Xavier, that must have been right around nine-twenty. But he didn't go into the office right away," Max said emphatically.

"I know," Keiko said, raising her eyebrows. "Is there something you are not telling me?"

Max told Keiko about the new witness that had turned up. "I don't know why someone would lie except to protect themselves. I wish I knew who it was. Jason wouldn't tell me even if he knew."

"You will figure something out," Keiko said.

Max refocused her attention on the timeline. "Between the time my dad followed the stranger out the back door and by the time he found the body it must have been about ten minutes."

"Because he found the body around nine-thirty?"

"Right."

Keiko took another look at her timeline. "That means that Xavier was killed between nine-ten and nine-thirty."

"That's about as good an estimate as we've got, and I bet it's as good as any the police have come up with."

"If the man your father saw leaving the office is the killer, then the time of death was nine-twenty or earlier."

"Exactly," Max agreed.

With the timeline as complete as possible, they returned their attention to the floor plan. She and Keiko wrote names on pieces of colored paper, and they spent the next hour reconstructing everyone's movements during the half hour before Richard found Xavier's body. Keiko drew little pictures for the strangers they couldn't identify.

Max pointed to one of Keiko's tiny people. "I remember that guy with the top hat. Oh, and there's Teresa with her silver braid." She looked closer. "Do my hips look that big in real life?"

Keiko sighed. "You may be losing focus on what is important."

"If you say so," Max said, disappointed that her joke hadn't even gotten a smile out of Keiko. "Plenty of these people had means and opportunity, but who had a motive?"

"That is an important question, now that you mention it," Keiko said. "I suppose Eliana had a motive if she were angry enough to kill Xavier, but we're pretty sure she couldn't lift the statue. What about Henry?"

The front door jingled, and a familiar voice called out, "Yoo, hoo! Anybody home?"

"Fiona," Keiko said. "Would you like me to get rid of her?"

"Actually, I've been hoping she'd show up soon. I called her earlier." Max called out, "We're in the back."

Fiona swooped in for air kisses with Max and Keiko, and then pulled up a stool.

Keiko jumped up. "Here, take my chair, it will be more comfortable."

"What a dear you are, Keiko," she said. "I'm doing well for my age, but I do appreciate a chair with some padding and back support."

"Are you here to spill the tea?" Keiko asked.

"What? I never spill tea. I wouldn't mind a cup, though, if you're offering."

"Spill the tea means to gossip," Keiko explained.

"It does? I like that. It's a nice way to put it, don't you think?"

"Whatever reason you're here, I'm glad you stopped by," Max said. "We were hoping you could help us reconstruct people's movements the night at the gallery."

"And see if you know something we don't," Keiko added.

Max told Fiona about the stranger her father saw leave the back of the gallery. "And now, a witness claims my dad went into the office ten minutes or so before he actually did." She forced herself to appear calm, or at least calmer than she felt.

Fiona froze. "But that means..."

"That means that my dad is a murder suspect."

Max stared at the paper in front of her. It made her feel better to do something, but what good would it do if someone were lying?

"The best way to keep my dad from being arrested is to find out who really killed Xavier."

CHAPTER 12

Fiona looked across the table, first at Max and then Keiko. "Okay, let's get to work, shall we? Who is your number one suspect?"

"Did you see anyone at the gallery wearing a fedora?"

"No, not that I recall," Fiona said. "Did your father get a good look at him?"

"No, unfortunately. He followed him out the back into the parking area, but then he lost him. I say him, but it could have been a her. My dad couldn't tell."

"That must be the murderer," Fiona concluded. "We just need to figure out who it was."

"Easier said than done," Keiko said.

"True," Max agreed. "And then there's Eliana. She had a major argument with Xavier right before he was killed."

"Really," Fiona said, leaning forward eagerly. "Tell me more."

Max recounted the argument she'd heard. "When Xavier and Eliana lowered their voices, I went looking for Keiko."

"Well, that's very interesting." Fiona picked up one of the colored pencils and began tapping it on the worktable. "So, we have the man in the fedora."

"Or woman," Max said.

"And we have Eliana. Perhaps she was angry enough to conk Xavier over the head." Fiona stopped tapping. "Do you think Eliana put on one of Xavier's fedoras after knocking him out and went out the back door?"

"It's possible," Keiko said. "Except the statue must have weighed nearly a hundred pounds."

"I see." Fiona considered this new information. "Eliana seems healthy and fit, but she doesn't appear strong enough to lift something that heavy. That means we're back to the man in the fedora, does it? We can safely say it's most likely a man, wouldn't you say?"

Max nodded in agreement. "We were hoping you could help us figure out who that might have been. What do you know about Xavier Hildalgo?"

"Ah, the victim. An excellent place to start." She hesitated. "If I'm going to spill the tea, as you say, perhaps we should get a pot of tea brewing. Nothing like a cuppa to get the old brain cells working."

Keiko jumped up from her stool. "Great idea. I'll start one." She slipped out of the room.

Fiona rambled on about what a lovely opening party it had been up until the murder, and how things had gotten much more interesting after that.

"Interesting?" Max questioned Fiona's choice of words.

"It's tragic, of course," Fiona corrected. "But I do find it interesting to watch how people react in a crisis. It can be exciting for those who don't know the victim, in the same way a good thriller is. I barely knew the man myself. I heard a lot of conjecture about who killed him, once people realized it was murder."

Max knew better than to trust gossip, but often a kernel of truth slipped in among the wild theories people discussed in whispers. "Who did people think might have wanted Xavier dead?"

Keiko appeared with the teapot, slipped out again, and returned moments later with three teacups and a bowl of sugar cubes.

"Yes." Keiko poured the first cup of tea. "What does the rumor mill have to say?"

"Well," Fiona began, looking like the cat that ate the canary. "One name that was mentioned more than a few times was Henry."

"Xavier's son?" Keiko asked.

"Everyone assumes he'll inherit everything since he's Xavier's only offspring."

"I spoke to him briefly last night," Max said, "Where is Henry's mother?"

"They've been divorced since Henry was a small child. It was a shotgun wedding just three months before Henry was born."

"What is a shotgun wedding?" Keiko asked.

Fiona laughed. "That's what they used to call it.

115

Having a baby out of wedlock would bring shame on a girl and her entire family. The father would hunt down the young man who was responsible and force him to get married, sometimes at gunpoint."

Keiko gasped. "Did that really happen?"

"It sure did. I don't know how often firearms were involved, but plenty of people got married just to avoid a scandal. And then with divorce often not an option, they were stuck with each other for life."

Keiko shook her head. "Boy, life was very different in the old days."

"Not to mention trying to keep the saber-tooth tigers from eating your young," Fiona deadpanned.

Keiko scrunched up her face and gave Fiona the side eye. "Now you are being funny, right?"

Fiona grinned, her eyes sparkling with mischief. "Maybe."

Max joined in. "If she tries to tell you that she only had one phone and it couldn't leave the house, don't believe her."

Keiko rolled her eyes. "I know all about land lines."

"Did you know that when you dialed the phone, you actually dialed?" Fiona mimicked dialing an old rotary phone.

Teresa appeared in the doorway. How had they not heard the door jingle? "Are you boring these young women with tales of olden times?"

"I was just going to tell them about my pet dinosaur."

Teresa whacked Fiona on the arm with her purse.

Luckily, the purse was on the small size, but Fiona rubbed her arm anyway.

"She was filling us in on Xavier and his ex-wife," Max explained.

"Ah yes," Teresa said. "They were both quite young at the time, especially... oh, what was her name?" Teresa paused and looked up at the ceiling, trying to remember. "Well, never mind. She was barely old enough to drive as I recall."

"And after the divorce, she moved to Los Angeles, and Xavier hardly ever saw his son as far as I could tell," Fiona added.

"I came to remind you of your doctor's appointment," Teresa said. "You're going to be late if you don't hightail it over there."

"The doctor? I thought that was tomorrow."

"The dentist is tomorrow. And you're not putting it off this time."

Fiona gave Max a long-suffering look. "Sisters," she said with a sigh. "They can be such a pain."

"Wait, Fiona," Max said. "Do we think Henry is the murderer?"

"I suppose it's possible, except for the fact that I saw him follow the paramedics in through the front door when they arrived."

Max sighed. "Why didn't you say so in the first place?"

"Where's the fun in that?" Fiona said, standing up. "See you girls later."

"Wait," Max said. "What was he doing out in front of the gallery in the middle of a showing?"

"I overheard Xavier ask him the same question," Fiona said. "When I heard the sirens stop in front of the gallery, I went to see what was going on. I saw the paramedics come in and Henry was right behind them. I think he was having a cigarette."

Teresa impatiently asked, "Are you coming?"

"Yes, yes," Fiona said. "Don't get your panties in a bunch."

"I'm going home, too," Keiko said. "I hope you are not planning to work very late tonight. It's going to be non-stop tomorrow. The day is fully booked."

"I know." Max was tired just thinking about another long day. "I just want to do a bit of sewing before I call it a night."

Max pulled out a chair in front of one of the sewing machines and remembered what Garrett had said about sewing being relaxing. Tonight was a good time to put that theory to the test.

"A package arrived. Did you see it?" Keiko asked. "I think it's the French silk tulle you were waiting for. How many yards did you order anyway?"

Max jumped up. "Thank goodness it's here. Daphne's first fitting is in one week. I can hand wash it tonight and it will be ready to sew on Sunday. Where is it?"

"How many yards?" Keiko repeated her question.

"Twenty yards," Max said. "I hope it's enough. I

guess it will have to be, since it takes so long for an order to get here."

"And why are you hand washing it?"

"To rinse out the sizing," Max explained. "You know how tulle is on the stiff side?" When Keiko nodded, she continued. "That's because of the sizing. Sizing is sort of like starch."

"I know what sizing is," Keiko said.

"Right. Of course, you do. I've gotten used to explaining everything with Heidi around. Well, you know how great tulle is for a tutu or a petticoat, but I want a softer flowy skirt for Daphne's gown."

Keiko walked over to a basket overflowing with hand-sewn flowers and picked one up to inspect. "And then you will sew these on, right?"

Max nodded. She'd been sewing the flowers for weeks, and there were at least fifty. "I hope there's enough. I'm tired of making them."

"I can stay and help with the washing if you want," Keiko offered.

"Thanks, but it shouldn't take long."

"Then I will see you tomorrow," Keiko said. "And the package is in the office."

"Great!" Max said. As soon as Keiko left, she wished she'd asked her to stay and help instead of being such a martyr. She didn't want to impose on their friendship, but boring tasks were always more tolerable and some-times even fun if you had company.

After she rinsed the tulle and hung it to dry, she

hurried home to talk with her father about his interview with Gallagher, or as her father called it, his interrogation. It was only nine o'clock, but the house was dark, and the doors were locked. She left her father a voice mail but fell asleep on her sofa waiting for him to call back.

The next morning, she saw a message from him. He would be out for the day but would talk to her that evening.

He seemed to be busy a lot lately, and she wondered if the friend he'd been with the night before was Eliana. The idea made her uneasy, but she shook off the feeling and got ready for work.

CHAPTER 13

When Max arrived at the shop early Saturday morning, she felt like she'd just left. It wasn't that far from the truth. She remembered telling Keiko it wouldn't take long to hand wash the silk tulle, but she'd decided it would be easier if she cut the skirt pieces first rather than trying to wash twenty yards of fabric all in one piece.

The tulle was draped all around the shop, over towel racks, chairs, and mannequins, and Max was happy to learn that it had dried overnight. She pulled the pieces down and folded them neatly in a stack.

The first bride they would be seeing that morning wanted an avant-garde wedding gown, according to Heidi. The bride had made the request when she made her appointment. Max wasn't exactly sure what she meant, but she prepared as best she could by pulling all the edgier and more daring gowns from the showroom and the overflow rack upstairs. She hung them outside one of the dressing rooms.

Heidi picked a good day to arrive early, considering their full schedule. "Hello, I'm here," she called out.

Max emerged from the dressing room area. "Good morning. We have a busy day today."

"What would you like me to do first?" Heidi asked.

"Let's go in the office and go over the appointment list," Max said. "You wrote a note next to the one o'clock appointment that said 'dog.'"

"Yes. She said she needed a dress for her dog."

"Is the dog getting married?" Max asked.

Heidi started to chuckle, and her chuckle became a guffaw. She seemed to think this was the funniest thing she'd heard in a while. Once she'd composed herself, she wiped a tear from her eye. "No, of course not. The dog is a bridesmaid."

Max stared at Heidi, trying to understand why a dog bride was hilarious while a dog bridesmaid was not. "We don't make dog dresses."

"But I do," Heidi said. "I'd be happy to make one to match the other bridesmaids' dresses. I mean, if it's okay with you."

"You make dog dresses?" Somehow this didn't surprise Max.

"Yes," Heidi said. "Well, usually costumes. You know. For Halloween and parades. Things like that. I told you how crafty I was when you interviewed me, remember?"

"Yes, I do. Well, from here on out, you are responsible for all the custom dog dress requests."

"Really?" Heidi clapped her hands in excitement and followed Max into the office. There was a new bounce in her step. Did she think dog dresses were going to be a regular thing at Wedding Belles? Max surely hoped not.

Heidi looked over Max's shoulder as she opened the appointment scheduling software. She was about to ask Heidi about a cryptic note next to one of the entries, when the front door gave a jingle, and Max heard a familiar voice.

"I'll get it," Heidi said.

"That's okay." Max stood up and headed back to the showroom. "I recognize that voice."

She opened the front door and was greeted with a big grin. "Hi, River." She stepped aside to let him enter. "I haven't seen you in ages."

Their mailman handed her several packages. "I spent two weeks at a meditation retreat," he said. "Just got back yesterday. Totally calmed my mind."

Max contemplated a calmer River than she was used to, but she couldn't imagine it. Everyone's favorite aging surfer was the most relaxed and reflective person she knew. "That's great, River."

"You look like you could use some serenity," River said. "And your aura is a bit cloudy."

"Cloudy?" That didn't sound like a good thing. "I've just been busy."

"Don't forget to breathe. 'Every breath we take can

be filled with peace, joy, and serenity.' That's a quote from Thich Nhat Hanh."

"Who?"

"You should totally check him out on YouTube," River said. "I can see the stress on your face."

That wasn't something Max wanted to hear having just turned thirty. She glanced at River's tan and lined face and observed smile lines around his eyes and mouth, but the space between his eyebrows showed not a single worry line. "Well, there's been a lot going on. You probably haven't heard."

"About the murder?" River asked. "I hear everything on my route, Max. I tune out the negativity as much as I can, but one must accept reality. The loss of life is always a tragedy, one that will come to each of us one day. I'm sorry your father's gallery opening had to end on a sad note."

"Yes. I'm worried about him. And the shop has been so busy that I have to work pretty much seven days a week. I knew owning a business would mean a lot of hard work, but I didn't realize I'd be working so many hours."

"Max," River said in a calm, quiet voice, "you must remember to work with love."

"Work with love?" Max felt a memory tug at her. "What does that mean?"

"The poet Khalil Gibran said it is 'to weave the cloth with threads drawn from your heart, even as if your beloved were to wear that cloth.'"

Max let his words sink in. "That's beautiful."

"And with that, I leave you to start your day. I believe your first appointment is here."

Sure enough, a petite, thirty-something woman entered. Was this the bride-to-be who wanted the avant-garde gown? She looked rather conservative in jeans and a gray sweatshirt.

"Good morning," Max said. "You must be Brittany. I'm Max." She watched as a spikey-haired platinum-blond man around the same age and an older woman, probably the bride's mother, followed her inside.

The petite woman began snickering. "I'm not getting married!" she said. "Marriage is an outdated institution designed to maintain the patriarchy."

Okay. This was going to be fun. "So..." Max turned toward the older woman.

"Brittany will be here in a moment," the woman said, and true to her word, a tall teenager slipped through the door. At least she looked like a teenager, with her limp, blonde hair and ripped jeans.

Max brought everyone into the Dream Room, so they could discuss what Brittany was looking for in a gown.

"I want something avant-garde," Brittany said. Her mother rolled her eyes, while the young man nodded.

"What about color?" Max asked. "Were you thinking white or off-white, or a more untraditional color?"

"You should get a black gown," the petite woman said. "You know, if you want something totally avant-garde."

"Yeah, yeah, yeah," the young man agreed. "That would literally blow everyone away."

"Do you have any black gowns?" Brittany asked.

"Yes, we do," Max said, but when she glanced at Brittany's mother, the woman shook her head. After spending half an hour helping Brittany try on dresses, and her mother vetoing every one, Max put her in a white princess gown with a lace veil. Brittany pretended to sulk, probably so her two friends wouldn't make fun of her, but Max could see the smile she tried to suppress.

Brittany's mother started to tear up the moment she saw her in the traditional wedding gown, and Max breathed a sigh of relief. The two friends protested, but mom had the final word. And Max knew that Brittany loved the gown, even if she wouldn't admit it.

At times like this, it seemed as if being a bridal consultant meant you needed to read people's minds. Max took Brittany's measurements and wrote up the order. Her mother told the three young people to wait for her outside.

"Thank you," she said. "I've been dreading this. Her friends are actually very nice young people, but they can be a bit of a handful."

"We were all that age once," Max said with a smile.

"True," she said. "I also wanted to thank you for making Crystal Shores a safer place to live."

"I don't understand," Max said.

"I think you do," the woman said. "I know this

murder wasn't here in town, but if you ask me, it was too close for comfort. Make sure you get the guy."

Max watched the woman hurry out the door. At least that was better than the woman at the party saying people were always dying around her.

Five hours, four appointments, and two pots of tea later, Max and Heidi put all the gowns back in their places and prepared for their last appointment.

"I'm going to need your help with this one," Max told Heidi. "Whether or not she orders her dress and her bridesmaids' dresses from us may depend on what she thinks of your plan for the dog's outfit."

Heidi's face lit up with delight. "I won't let you down. I appreciate the confidence you're showing in me."

Heidi's enthusiasm was starting to grow on Max. She was normally distrustful of people who showed an overabundance of eagerness, but Heidi seemed sincere. Her effusiveness contrasted with Keiko's reserve so completely, sometimes they left Max feeling off balance.

The dog turned out to be a tiny ball of fluff named Snowflake. The Pomeranian was adorable, but it was nearly impossible to try on dresses when the woman wouldn't put the dog down, and besides, it kept trying to nip at Max.

Heidi helped by cooing at the dog and complimenting it endlessly. Snowflake soon calmed down and even allowed Heidi to hold her, which made the rest of the appointment go much more smoothly. Max half expected the bride-to-be to ask Heidi to take over, they were bonding so well, but thankfully that didn't happen. As much as Heidi wanted to be a full-blown bridal consultant, it would be some time before she would be ready to work with clients on her own.

After the woman picked out the perfect gown, Heidi took over. She took Snowflake's measurements and promised to have the tiny dress done so the bride and her dog could have their first fitting together.

THE EVENINGS WERE BEGINNING TO GET CHILLY, AND Max zipped up her new jacket and hurried home. An intoxicating scent drifted in the night air and then disappeared. Even the night-blooming jasmine was confused by the warm weather they'd had lately.

She stopped for a moment in front of the house she'd grown up in. A huge hedge hid the front entrance. Behind one dormer window was her second-floor bedroom, and through the curtains she could see her old four-poster bed with its white lace canopy.

The path along the side of the house led to the cozy backyard that was more of a patio than a yard. Max climbed the stairs to her apartment over the garage and unlocked the security screen door her father had installed last year. Fiona was right. The world had changed, and Max wasn't always sure it was for the better.

After changing into a sweatshirt and jeans, she walked down the steps and through the back door of her father's house so they could finally have their talk. The kitchen was empty, and she didn't smell anything cooking, which was disappointing. No one in the living room, either.

"Dad?"

"I'm in the studio," he called back.

The studio was once one of the downstairs bedrooms, refitted with additional windows to provide more natural light. When they'd first moved in, he'd pulled up the carpet revealing the original hardwood, but he refused to refinish it, saying if he did, he'd have to worry about getting paint on it. Max loved to paint and do crafts in this room as a child because no one got mad if you spilled something.

"Hi, Dad, I—" she began, before she realized he had company.

"Hi, Hon. You remember Eliana." Her father sat on a stool in front of his easel, while Eliana stood next to him. "I was just showing her how the painting was coming."

"Nice to see you." Max forced a smile.

"Nice to see you too, Max," she replied.

"Well, I just wanted to check in on you, after, you know." She didn't want to talk about the new witness in front of Eliana. "I'll leave you alone to, um, talk, or whatever." Why did she feel so awkward? It's not like she hadn't seen her dad with other women before.

"We're going to Chez Mer for dinner," Richard said. "Want to join us?"

"Um, no," she replied quickly. "Thanks, but I have plans. See you later."

She practically ran out of the room before her dad could tell she was lying. It was just a white lie, right? So why did she feel so guilty?

Back in her apartment, she sat on the sofa considering ordering a pizza. It was funny how Keiko had accused her of never having time for her friends, and here she was with a free evening and no one to spend it with. It seemed as though everyone had gotten used to her not being available.

Feeling lonely and a bit needy, she thought about calling Jason, but the hurt she felt from his decision to move away was too fresh. They would need to have a long talk about their relationship, but it didn't have to be tonight.

If only she had someone to bounce ideas off of. It was hard to investigate on her own, and she had to admit she'd reached a dead end. The marble statue was almost certainly too heavy for Eliana to lift, and Henry was seen in front of the gallery just after the murder. That left the guy or gal in the fedora, whoever that might be.

Her stomach growled and she had a brilliant thought. Burt usually worked at The Crazy Fox on Saturdays. Bartenders never minded when you dropped in unannounced. Bartenders were cool that way. Plus, Burt knew all the businesses in town. Maybe he could tell her where to find marble statues. Keiko was amazing at research, but sometimes you could learn more in person.

After changing out of her sweatshirt into something more presentable, she walked the four blocks to the restaurant, thinking about what she would order. Food didn't solve problems, but it sure made her feel better. And a glass of wine wouldn't hurt either.

CHAPTER 14

*B*urt looked up when Max stepped into the bar. "Hey, Max! Good to see you."

"Hi, Burt. Got a spot at the bar?"

"For you?" He grinned. "Always, even if I have to kick out one of these stool warmers." He turned to two regulars at the far end of the bar. "No offense."

"None taken," a man in a tan polo shirt answered. "Keeping bar stools warm is one of my best talents."

Max found an empty seat and grabbed the happy hour menu. Half price appetizers until seven. "What time is it?"

"Five minutes to seven," Burt answered. "Want me to put in an order before happy hour ends?"

"Yes, please." Max added a glass of house wine to her order, also half price. "I need to come here more often."

"I agree," Burt said with a smile as he pulled a wine glass from the mirrored shelf behind him. "Are you planning to have more than one glass of wine? The price goes up in a few minutes."

"Just one will do." Max watched as he filled the wine glass a bit fuller than the normal amount. "You don't happen to know anyone who sells marble busts, do you?"

"Thinking of redecorating? I would have pegged you as mid-century modern or perhaps shabby chic."

Max made a face. She actually loved shabby chic, but she would never admit it. "I just need to know how heavy a marble bust weighs." It's not that she doubted Keiko's research, but sometimes you could get more information face to face.

"I see." Burt leaned forward, his elbows on the bar. "Asking for a friend?"

Max grinned and put on her best innocent face. "Exactly."

"Hey, Joe," Burt called out to the man in the polo shirt who had spoken moments before. "Do you know how heavy marble is?"

"A marble bust," Max clarified.

Joe seemed pleased to have been brought into the conversation. "Hi, I'm Joe," he told Max unnecessarily.

"Uh, huh," she said. "I'm Max."

"Max. Is that short for—"?

"Don't go there," Burt cautioned, winking at Max. "Joe owns Elegant Furnishings, the interior design shop two blocks up from here."

Joe returned to the subject at hand. "How tall is this marble bust?"

"About a foot tall, maybe a little bigger." She held her hands up to show the size. "I think it was a Greek god or something like that." Max thought for a moment before she remembered the name. "It was Hermes."

"Ah, mischievous Hermes. He's not one of the more popular ones. Most people want Zeus or Aphrodite."

"Any idea how heavy it would be?" Max asked, trying not to let her impatience show.

"Nearly a hundred pounds, I'd guess."

"Wow, that heavy?" She doubted Eliana could lift that much even if she were in a rage. "I guess that changes things. Thanks, Joe."

"Sure thing. You seem disappointed."

"No, not disappointed. It just changes things a bit."

Joe nodded in understanding. "Marble is beautiful and classic, but it's not always practical."

"Uh, huh," Max said absentmindedly.

"You've obviously got your heart set on one you've seen somewhere. Maybe I can find you something similar. Perhaps a smaller bust."

"What?" It took a moment for Max to understand what he was getting at. "Oh, no. I'm not looking for one for myself."

"For a friend then," Joe said knowingly. "I see."

Max didn't bother correcting him. She didn't want to explain that the bust she was interested in was not a potential gift but a murder weapon.

She reached for her wine glass, not wanting to get involved in a long conversation with this stranger, even if he had been very helpful. Keiko was right. Eliana couldn't possibly pick up anything that heavy. The murderer must have been a very strong man.

"Of course, they do wonderful things with resin these days. You can hardly tell the difference. I mean, you can hardly put a ninety-pound bust on a bookcase, now, can you?" He laughed as if this was a silly thought.

Max stopped mid sip and straightened up. "No. You can't. Tell me about resin, Joe."

Joe grinned, happy to be able to further share his expertise. Before the evening was over, Max knew way more than she ever wanted about the weight of every material used to make faux marble busts. Resin was heavy enough to conk someone on the head with and solid enough that it wouldn't shatter in the process. It was also light enough that a woman could easily lift it.

By the time she said goodnight to Burt and Joe, she was elated about what she'd learned, but stepping out into the cool night air, she remembered the way her father looked at Eliana. She had felt disappointed when she'd thought Eliana was innocent and pleased to put her back on the list.

"Just because you don't trust her, doesn't mean she's a murderer," Max muttered to herself as she waited for a break in the traffic, so she could cross Coast Highway.

THE LIGHT WAS ON WHEN SHE REACHED HOME. SHE STILL considered it her home, even though she lived over the garage now.

Out of habit, she went around the rear of the house and entered through the back door, hoping to catch her father alone. They hadn't had a chance to talk since Gallagher had told him about the supposed witness.

She closed the door noiselessly and slipped in quietly through the kitchen. Turning the corner, she saw him on the sofa with a book. A memory rushed in, and she pictured her mother and father sitting reading on that same sofa while she curled up in the easy chair with her own book. Funny how some memories could make you happy and sad at the same time.

Her dad looked up. "Hi, Sunshine. I didn't hear you come in."

"I didn't want to disturb you if you were busy."

He chuckled knowingly. "Eliana is just a friend."

Max hesitated for a moment. "A friend who you're in love with?" She said it as a question, hoping her instincts were wrong, just this once.

Richard closed his book and set it aside. "Is it that obvious?"

"It is to me. But then I know you better than anyone. I've seen you with other women you've dated, and you look at her differently." When he didn't say anything, she asked, "How long?" She didn't finish the question, wanting him to fill in the blanks.

"I only just figured it out for myself, and I haven't told her how I feel, so don't you go saying anything. I don't think she's ready for another relationship just yet." He paused, and then added, "And I never looked at another woman while your mother was alive."

Max nodded. She knew her father would never have been disloyal to her mother.

"I know you don't care for Eliana," Richard said. "You know no one could ever replace your mother, right?"

"It's not that. It's just..." She told him about the argument she'd overheard between Eliana and Xavier. Against her better judgement, she added, "She might be a murderer."

Richard didn't even try to look surprised. "She's not," he said. "Just because we were the last people to see Xavier, doesn't mean either of us murdered him."

"How do you know he was still alive after she talked to him?"

"How do you know I didn't do it?" he asked calmly. "Gallagher seems to think I might be guilty."

"Well—" How was she supposed to answer that question? "I know you."

"And I know Eliana."

This conversation was going nowhere. Richard told her more about his interview with Gallagher the previous day, but he wasn't able to tell her any more than she already knew.

Max felt her phone vibrate. It was a text from Jason asking if he could stop by. "Do you have any wine?" she asked Richard.

"Sure. Want me to pour you a glass?"

"Actually, I wanted it to go."

Richard raised one eyebrow. "There's a bottle in the kitchen. You know where I keep it."

Jason knocked on the door of her apartment. He must have been nearby when he texted her to get there so fast. After an awkward moment, Jason gave her a kiss on the cheek, and followed Max to the living room. He sat in an easy chair across from her.

"I need to know who the witness is who says he saw my dad," Max said.

"I don't know who it is," he said. "I can't interfere with Detective Gallagher's investigation, you know that, right? I could lose my job."

"You're not planning to stay at this job anyway."

He ignored her comment. "We'll do things by the book."

"Oh, no." Max stood up and put her hands on her hips, feeling suddenly invincible. "You need to do things by the book. I just need to make sure no one gets hurt or fired. Except for one person. Someone is a murderer, and they're going down." She turned to walk out the room dramatically and tripped over the ottoman. "Darn it."

In the kitchen, she pondered her options. It was so confusing working with a police detective who wasn't actually on the case and who also was her boyfriend. At least she hoped he was still her boyfriend, but for how long?

She got the bottle of wine out of the refrigerator, poured two glasses, and returned to the living room.

Jason took the glass from her. "Can we talk? About us, I mean?"

Max sat down next to him. "I don't know what to say. When are you moving?"

"I haven't accepted the job yet. The police chief wants me to fly out and meet with the hiring committee before he makes me an official offer."

"Then I guess we should talk when you come back," Max said.

Jason took her hand in his and stroked it gently. "We can figure this out, Max. We'll make it work."

When Max didn't respond, he stood to go. "I'll let you get some rest. It's late."

He gave her another kiss on the cheek and left. She closed the door after him wondering what had happened to her great love affair. Did he really love her? If he did, why would he even consider leaving?

CHAPTER 15

*M*ax took one step out of her apartment and into the chilly morning air. "Brr." It sure had cooled off since the previous week, and it looked like it might rain.

She went back inside and dug through her closet and drawers until she found her umbrella along with a knit hat, scarf, and two gloves. They didn't match, but at least they would be warm. Feeling more prepared for her short walk to work, she headed down the stairs.

She looked longingly at her father's kitchen window. If he was up, he would probably make her pancakes, but she wanted to get a head start on the day. She had packed a granola bar in her purse, and it would have to do.

With Garrett helping during the week, she had a chance of catching up on her custom gown orders, but that didn't mean she could take it easy. She walked around the side of the house to the front and headed down the sidewalk past white picket fences and flowering gardens. The residents of Crystal Shores wouldn't allow a little thing like winter keep them from enjoying their colorful displays. Strolling leisurely past the pastel cottages, she stopped to smell a neighbor's gardenia when it started to drizzle. She opened her umbrella and picked up her pace.

The back door of the shop opened into the sewing room. It was also the storage room and receiving area, and a dozen newly arrived wedding gowns covered in heavy plastic hung in one corner of the room. Steaming them and finding a spot for them upstairs would be a job for Heidi on Monday.

The shop was chilly, but Max didn't want to heat up the whole place when she was the only one there, so she pulled out the radiant heater she'd bought last winter. It warmed up quickly, and she stood in front of it, rotating like a rotisserie chicken to take the chill out of her bones.

Max kept her custom projects in order by assigning each a drawer in a large dresser. She pulled open the drawer which held all the materials and trims for Daphne's dress. It seemed as if Eric's assistant's budget had no limit, and she wanted the best of everything. With a daddy who obliged her every whim, the best was what she would be getting.

The ivory silk bodice had been hand painted by a local artist, and the effect was breathtaking. The chiffon flowers Max had created and dyed pale pink to match the bodice were ready to be sewn, one by one, onto the French silk tulle skirt.

Next to the dresser stood their supply hutch. Once she had pulled on her sewing apron with its roomy and practical pockets, Max opened the hutch's doors, revealing dozens of spools of thread, most in shades of white and off-white. She said a silent thank you to Keiko for organizing them along with the pins, needles, and other supplies.

For this task, she needed green embroidery floss, which would be the center of each flower, and an embroidery needle.

She reached into the pockets of her apron for her favorite thimble, but as quite often happened, it had gone missing. She chastised herself for being so absent-minded.

After a few minutes, Max gave up and retrieved a brand-new leather thimble, which would be stiff until she broke it in, but it would do. She plopped down in the comfy armchair she kept in the corner. It was faded and worn, but somehow it was just right for curling up in when she had hand sewing to do. She had a thought, stood back up, and pulled up the cushion. There was her old thimble.

"Hello, old friend," she said, glad that no one was around to witness her talking to a thimble.

After she made herself comfortable, she began to stitch the flowers onto the tulle, attaching a small piece of interfacing to the back to stabilize it and keep the flowers from tearing away from the delicate fabric.

As she sewed, she thought about the witness her father had told her about. If Gallagher believed them, it made her father look guilty, especially if Gallagher thought he'd lied about the man in the fedora.

"Why would they lie?" Max asked herself. She couldn't imagine anyone wanting to frame her dad. And then it hit her.

The witness had to be the murderer or perhaps even an accomplice. That was the only thing that made sense.

She took stitch after stitch, thinking about how to find out the identity of the secret witness, convinced it would tell her who killed Xavier. She needed to talk to Randy, otherwise known as Officer Rivera. He might not be willing to disclose the information, but she had to try.

She attached the last flower and stood up to get a look at her handiwork, pleased with the final result. She twirled around with the skirt and grinned at the way the flowers seemed to float on top of the layers of tulle. The fantasy princess wedding gown Daphne had asked for was coming along beautifully. Now it was time to attach the skirt to the bodice.

Max felt a pang in her stomach. It must be time for lunch, and she'd completely forgotten about the granola bar that was supposed to have been her breakfast. It looked like it would be her lunch instead.

A nice cup of tea would make it more of a meal, she figured. She sat down with her tea and granola bar, and dialed Randy's number, hoping he hadn't changed it over the past couple of years.

She left Randy a message, and it was hours later before he called back. He sounded pleased to hear from her, but not as pleased when Max asked him about the witness. "I don't think I'm supposed to tell anyone," he said.

"I understand," Max said, not about to give up that easily. "How about getting together for lunch tomorrow? Or a drink after work?"

Randy paused before answering, sounding reluctant. "Actually, Detective Gallagher told me not to talk to you at all, so I don't think I should. Maybe after the investigation is closed?" he added hopefully.

"Sure," Max said, admitting defeat. "I'll call you."

Feeling deflated, Max decided to call it a day. Every muscle in her back and shoulders ached from sitting in one position for so long. She hadn't planned to work a twelve-hour day and wondered how long she could keep up this pace, not to mention survive on a diet of granola bars and pizza.

The clouds had all but disappeared, and she walked home under a starry sky fantasizing about a spa day with a long massage, maybe with hot stones or essential oils or something decadent like that.

In spite of her best efforts, the gown wasn't finished. Daphne's appointment for her first fitting was scheduled for Friday. That was just five days away. She hoped with Garrett's help she'd get it done on time.

She slept fitfully, dreaming about sewing and

ripping out stitches with the dreaded seam ripper. A nightmare woke her up, and she squinted at the clock. Midnight. She tossed and turned and tossed some more before giving up and getting out of bed.

The empty refrigerator mocked her with its half empty mustard and a piece of moldy cheese. A cup of herbal tea might help calm her mind, but she felt restless. She decided a short walk and some fresh air was what she needed. She loved living in a place safe enough to walk any time of the day or night. There might be murders in Crystal Shores, but no one was attacking random people in the street, and she hoped it stayed that way.

She pulled on a sweatshirt over the yoga pants and t-shirt she slept in and slipped into sneakers. It was nearly one o'clock when she crept down the stairs, and the light was on in her father's studio. He often painted well into the night when he felt inspired.

She turned toward the alley and followed it toward the ocean. For a moment, she considered going back to her warm bed, but she knew the sea breeze and the sounds of the waves crashing on the beach would calm her mind. Hopefully, when she did crawl back into bed, she'd sleep more peacefully.

She wasn't sure if she'd planned to walk to Eliana's house, but that's where she found herself several minutes later. A single light glowed through the curtains, and she saw movement. Or maybe it was just a flickering candle. She took a few steps closer to get a better look, staying close to the next-door neighbor's hedge in case someone nosy happened to be looking out their window.

Two silhouettes could be seen through the curtain, one taller than the other. Okay, Eliana had a friend over. She was allowed.

Then the two shadows merged in an embrace. A long embrace. Max took a few more steps but if she moved any closer, she'd have to step out in the open, and she really didn't want to have to explain to anyone what she was doing outside Eliana's house at one in the morning.

The light in the house went out and Max was still wondering what she'd just seen when an upstairs light went on.

She started to walk away but turned back when the most likely explanation hit her like a brick. The man she'd just seen with Eliana must have been her father. His car wasn't parked outside, but that could mean that he wanted their relationship to be a secret. Why would he lie to her?

Max woke up Monday morning with a start. Her phone buzzed and vibrated on the nightstand with a text from Jason. Wondering why he was bothering her so early, she saw the time and leapt out of bed. She was meeting Garrett at nine, and she'd have to hurry if she was going to get there in time.

It took her a moment to realize that her middle of the night walk hadn't been a dream. She didn't have time to think about it right now or answer Jason's text. Soon she was dressed and presentable, with her hair in a messy bun that she hoped looked fashionable and not just, well, messy.

By the time she got to the shop, she found herself with ten minutes to spare, so she checked her calendar and started a small pot of coffee. She might need two cups today after her limited sleep the night before.

Garrett arrived right on time, as expected, and handed her a cup from Rose's cafe. "Don't expect this every morning. I just wanted to get on my new boss's good side. I'm told cappuccinos are your favorite."

Max grinned. "Thank you, they are. Shall we get started?"

"Ah yes, you're a busy woman with no time for small talk. I remember how it was when I ran a business."

Max walked Garrett back to the workroom. "On Mondays, we're open by appointment only, so I get a fair amount of sewing done if Heidi or Keiko are here to answer phones and handle walk-in customers."

"I see," Garrett said. "Why do you have walk-ins if you're not open?"

Max laughed. "If you come in on a Monday, the only thing you can do is make an appointment."

"I see. You don't leave the door locked?"

Max eyed him with interest. "Do you think I should keep the door locked?"

"It's not my shop. It's your decision." He walked over to the Bernina. "I watched some online tutorials on this machine over the weekend, and I think I have a handle on it now. Will you be sewing this morning as well?"

"Yes. I thought for your first day I would walk you through how I do things, and then I'll be working in here with you so you can ask as many questions as you want. Are you familiar with French seams?"

"That's when you sew wrong sides together first and then the right sides, correct?"

"Yes," Max answered, pleased that he was so knowledgeable. "I use them for any unlined sections. I like the inside to look almost as beautiful as the outside. People spend a lot of money for a custom gown, and they deserve the best craftsmanship I can provide."

"That is a refreshing attitude, Max."

Max pulled Daphne's dress off the rack and looked it over, making sure each flower had been sewn on perfectly. She had to admit, the effect was delightful, as if the flowers were floating on top of the gown.

"Is this one of your designs?" Garrett asked, stepping closer to get a better look.

"Yes," she answered. "What do you think?"

She watched him as he looked at the gown from every angle, nervously waiting for his opinion.

He finally spoke. "Delightful. Simply delightful. The details are exquisite, and the workmanship is impeccable. It's almost a work of art."

Max beamed. "Thank you." It meant a lot coming from him, with his decades in the fashion industry.

"Do you enjoy making one-of-a-kind gowns, Max?"

Max grinned. "I love creating them, but it is a lot of

work. They are quite lucrative, but sometimes I wonder if there are better uses of my time."

Garrett nodded knowingly. "I don't know how attached you are to this little shop, but if you wanted to branch out and start your own line, I would be happy to connect you to the right people."

"Really?" Max had dreamed of having her own fashion line someday, but she thought she'd given up that dream when she chose to stay in Crystal Shores instead of moving to New York.

"I hope you don't mind me saying your current business model doesn't appear to be sustainable for the long term. At some point, you may have to make a choice between running a bridal shop and designing gowns."

Max had never looked at it that way. "You may have a point."

"We can talk more later, if you like. Hopefully, I don't end up talking myself out of a job. I'm looking forward to coming here every morning and getting to know you and Keiko better."

Garrett sat down at the sewing machine and began to work, and Max assumed that meant they were done talking for now.

Garrett had a point about leaving the door locked on Mondays, so she didn't unlock the front door at ten as she usually did. She worked at the cutting table while he sewed without interruption for nearly an hour.

She couldn't believe how lucky she was to find

Garrett, although she reminded herself, he was the one who found her. And it seemed that she'd found a mentor as well.

She didn't hear the front door jingle, so she was surprised to hear a voice call out, "Hello? Anyone home?"

Keiko was just the person she wanted to talk to. "I'll be in the showroom if you need me," she told Garrett. "You should take a break, even if it's just a quick stretch."

"There you are," Keiko said when Max emerged from the workroom. "The front door was locked. I had to use my key."

"Yes, it's something new I'm trying on Mondays."

"It's about time," Keiko said. "Any appointments for today?"

"There's one at eleven and another at one. Heidi should be here shortly to help. Before she gets here, can we talk? I need you to tell me if I'm crazy or not."

"You're crazy," Keiko said.

"No, that's not what I meant."

"Okay, you're not crazy?"

Max chuckled in spite of herself. "I think my father and Eliana are having an affair." She told Keiko about the man she'd seen through Eliana's window the previous night.

"Are you sure it was your father?" Keiko asked.

Max considered the idea for a moment. "Do you think she might be seeing someone else besides my dad?"

"It's possible. Remember when we saw her at the Crazy Fox before your party? She seemed...how should I say this? Friendly? I would not put it past her to be seeing more than one person."

"You might be right, but when I got home after one, my dad's studio light was still on, and the rest of the house was dark."

"Then he was working late in his studio," Keiko suggested.

"I looked through the windows, and he wasn't in there," Max said. "He never leaves the lights on. Ever."

"You are peeping through a lot of windows lately."

Max grimaced. "It's not something I normally do, trust me." As much as she wanted to believe the man Eliana was with was not her father, her gut told her otherwise. "If my dad was with Eliana, why is he hiding it from me?"

Max tried to resolve all the thoughts and feelings going through her head. "I need to find out more about Eliana. My dad is so trusting, and I've never seen him fall hard for someone like this. I don't want him to get hurt."

Keiko grinned. "Just give me an hour with the computer."

"Thanks, Keiko," Max said, as Keiko made a beeline for the office.

$\mathcal{M}$ax surveyed the long row of wedding gowns that took up one wall. There were more upstairs, but Max kept the latest arrivals here along with any that had been featured in a bridal magazine. The look of delight when a bride-to-be held out a picture from the latest issue, and she was able to pull the exact gown from the rack, never ceased to bring her joy.

The bride-to-be who was coming in that morning was a referral from Eric's assistant Daphne, and Max knew nothing else about her. She always felt a touch of nerves when she didn't know what to expect, but that feeling almost always disappeared after meeting an excited, new bride-to-be.

The door jingled and Heidi burst through. "I'm sorry I'm late," she said, panting. "I got a call from one of the moms complaining to me that her kid didn't get chosen for the school talent show and I couldn't get off the phone. I finally put her on speakerphone so I could get dressed."

Max smiled at her harried new assistant. "Part of the reason I hired you was because you were president of the PTA. I figured if you could handle difficult Crystal Shores parents, our clients would be a breeze. I also knew that with two kids, you would need some flexibility. As long as you're just a few minutes late, I don't have a problem."

"Thanks." Heidi took a deep breath and let it out slowly. "You are so understanding. I got fired at my last job the second time I showed up late. I mean, I had missed a couple of days of work because Michael had strep throat. Boy, that kid was so miserable. It was so painful for him to swallow, and he got tired of eating ice cream. Can you imagine getting tired of eating ice cream? I don't think I ever would."

"Shall we get to work?" Max suggested before Heidi could provide more details.

It turned out that their first appointment had been to four different bridal shops before she had been referred to Wedding Belles. Luckily, Max didn't know this until after the client had chosen a gown and put in her order. Not only was the bride happy, her mother was in tears, and Max guessed they were tears of relief that she didn't have to accompany her daughter to any more shops.

After the bride left, Max checked in with Garrett. His work was impeccable, but he hadn't listened to her when she told him to stretch. He stood up stiffly.

"Every hour," Max said firmly. "You need to stand up and do a few stretches. I find I get so focused, that I almost forget to move. And try both chairs to see which one is most comfortable for you. Or we can get you another chair. You're bigger, I mean, taller than me."

Garrett chuckled. "You can say bigger. I have a wonderful and very expensive ergonomic chair I brought home from the office when I retired. I'll bring it in tomorrow if that's okay with you."

"Of course. Keiko is picking up sandwiches. Would you like her to pick you up something? I can send her a text."

"I think I'll call it a day, if that's all right with you. I'll bring the chair in tomorrow and remember to take breaks."

"I'm very grateful you're here," Max said.

"Thank you," Garrett replied. "I can't remember the last time one of my bosses said anything so nice to me. Of course, I was the boss for the past decade, so I suppose I have no one to blame but myself." He grinned. "See you tomorrow."

"Wait a moment. I have something for you" she said. Keiko had done such thorough research on their new employee that she knew she could trust him completely. She came back with a spare key. "This way you can come in at nine like you wanted to. No need to wait for me to get here."

"Thank you, Max," he said, taking the key. "I appreciate that. I'm an early riser, and at my age, it's hard to change those habits."

When Keiko returned with the sandwiches, Heidi went upstairs to steam and organize the newly arrived gowns, while Keiko and Max convened in the workroom. "Here is what I found out," Keiko began as she unwrapped her avocado sandwich, "Eliana and Leo were married five years ago in Bolivia. She, it turns out, comes from a very wealthy family. They helped Leo promote his paintings and other artwork, hiring an expensive New York public relations firm and using their connections to get him gallery shows all over the world."

Max was about to take a bite of her sandwich, but put it back down, fascinated by Keiko's story. "I remember he did seem to burst on the scene out of nowhere."

Keiko checked her notes. "Unfortunately, he spent money like it was going out of style. He was known as a high roller at the best casinos in Las Vegas."

"He could afford it, couldn't he? His original paintings sell for the tens of thousands, and who knows how much he makes on all the prints and merchandise."

"The corporation was doing very well, but his in-laws had control of it. He had a six-figure salary, but his spending went way beyond his means. The hotels and casinos gave him credit, thinking he was wealthy, but he really wasn't."

"Wow." Max was once again impressed by Keiko's research skills. She must have done some digging to get so much information so quickly. "So did Eliana bail him out?"

"Eliana's wealth is held in a trust. Even if she wanted to help him, she didn't have access to that kind of money. She gets a very generous allowance, and she and her three siblings will inherit everything eventually, but Leo was in debt to the tune of nearly a million dollars."

Max let out a low whistle. "That's a lot of cabbage."

Keiko nodded. "A whole lot of cabbage that went away when he died."

"Hmmm…" Max had just taken a bite of her pastrami melt, so she couldn't say much more. The wheels in her head began to turn. "I remember hearing that Leo's plane crashed off the coast of Baja California, Mexico. Was his body ever found?"

"It was not," Keiko said. "Why? What are you thinking?"

"If Leo had faked his death, it would have been a brilliant con game. His original artwork had doubled in value." Max sat back in her chair, pondering what all these clues added up to.

"It's really hard to fake your own death," Keiko said. "Especially if you owe money to some sketchy characters. They'd want to be sure he was dead, and if not, they would track him down."

"I hate it when you punch holes in my crazy theories. Plus, he had a wife to think about."

"That is not as much of an issue," Keiko said. "Eliana had filed for divorce shortly before he died."

"What?" Max stood up so quickly she nearly knocked over her stool.

Heidi stuck her head in the door. "Your one o'clock appointment is here."

"Thanks, Heidi," Max wished she had more time to talk with Keiko about Eliana and Leo and decide if this new information was important. She motioned to Heidi to come into the workroom. "Why don't you take a break? One of those oatmeal chocolate chip cookies is for you."

"It is?" Heidi ran up to Max and grabbed her in a hug, while Keiko shrugged as if to say, "Well, you hired her."

CHAPTER 17

*M*ax plopped down in one of the sage green easy chairs in the showroom. Two days in a row of nearly constant sewing had exhausted her. She rolled her shoulders and leaned her head side to side to stretch out the stiff muscles.

In the little girl voice Heidi used when she wanted something, she said, "Um, would it be okay if I went home? I mean, I know I'm supposed to stay until five on Mondays, but—"

"Go ahead," Max said with a wave of her hand. "We can handle things here."

"We?" Keiko cocked her head as if she must have misunderstood.

"I can handle things," she corrected. "Have a good evening, and I'll see you tomorrow."

"Um, about tomorrow. Can I come in a little later, like noon? I looked at the schedule and you don't have any appointments until after lunch. I can work until six if you want because—"

"Yes," Keiko said, shooing her out the door. "Now go."

"Thank you!" Heidi practically skipped out the door, but before she was out of earshot, they heard her say, "Hello! Yes, she's inside."

Jason stepped through the door, and Max's heart almost stopped beating. She didn't often see him in a suit these days, and it took her right back to the first time she'd met him. It was in a hospital waiting room right after a bride-to-be had collapsed in her shop. Not the most romantic way to meet, she had to admit, but for Max it was love at first sight, or at the very least, a very strong attraction.

Keiko appeared with her bag over her shoulder. "I'm going next door to meet with Fiona and Teresa. Stop by later if you want." She swept out the door without waiting for an answer

Max invited Jason to sit down in one of the overstuffed chairs, but he shook his head.

"Can we go for a walk?" Before she could answer, he added, "It's a beautiful afternoon and the sun will be setting soon."

"But the shop," Max began.

"Is closed on Mondays," he said, "except for appointments, isn't it?"

"Yes, it is." Walking side by side might be less awkward than she felt standing here with him in the bright lights of her shop. "Let me grab my jacket."

They walked past The Knitpickers yarn store and the bakery, and when they turned on Daffodil Street the ocean lay ahead of them, sparkling in the bright sun that hung low in the sky. Sailboats lazily made their way back to the harbor.

As they walked, Max filled him in on Keiko's research and her theory that Leo Baldassari might not really be dead.

"I have to say, that's not the craziest theory I've ever heard, but it's a contender."

"He was in a huge amount of debt, and now, if he's alive and he's taken over another identity, he can start over."

"It's not easy to fake your own death," Jason said.

"I know," Max said, disappointed. "Keiko said the same thing. But, it's not impossible, right?"

Jason just shook his head, no doubt marveling at her stubbornness. "I learned something I thought you might want to hear. I got this information without using my credentials or access, but I don't want to have to explain that to anyone." He turned to her and added softly, "Well, anyone but you."

"Got it."

"Henry says he did head for the office to talk to his father, but when he heard Eliana and Xavier arguing, he decided not to interrupt them. He went out front and only came back in after the paramedics arrived."

"I know. Fiona saw him. But Henry could be lying. He might have gone in the office after Eliana came out and knocked his dad over the head. There was time."

"I don't know about that," Jason said. "The gallery was wall-to-wall people. It would take a while to get to the front door. Do you think he has a motive to kill his father?"

"I have no idea. I have another theory," she said. "I think the witness who said my dad went into the office earlier than he really did is most likely the murderer. Was it Henry?"

"That I don't know," Jason said.

"And if you did know, you couldn't tell me."

"I'm sorry, Max." Jason said, his voice barely more than a whisper. "I know it looks bad right now, but remember, your dad doesn't have a motive."

"Oh," Max brightened. "I hadn't thought of that. That's good, right?"

"Yes, that's good," he said.

They walked in silence until they reached the end of the street where a narrow stretch of grass ended in a small cliff. In her younger years, she scrambled down it to what she considered her own private beach. The sun slowly sank below the horizon turning the sky vivid shades of pink and orange. She felt as if she were being pounded the way the waves pounded the sand on the beach below them.

"I'm here for you," Jason said, sitting down next to her. "Whatever you need."

Max reached for his hand, and he seemed relieved by the small gesture. What she really needed was for him to stay by her side and not move to Miami. But right now, she was tired of talking. "I'm hungry."

Jason laughed. "Of course, you are. You're the only person I know who constantly eats and never puts on weight."

Max thought about how nearly half of her closet had become "skinny" clothes that she hoped to fit into again one day but didn't bother to contradict him.

"I'll take you to that Indian place you love," he suggested.

She answered with a stomach growl but shook her head. "I want to swing by the Knitpickers. Keiko said she was stopping in, and I want to find out if she's learned anything new."

Max could see his disappointment, but she didn't care. She wasn't the one who was putting her career before their relationship. Or was she? Life was so complicated.

Max stopped in at her shop to grab her purse from the office before walking next door to the Knitpickers Yarn Shop. She tried the door, but it was locked. She knocked firmly, and a voice called out, "Come in! It's not locked!"

"Yes, it is," she called back.

A few moments later Fiona pulled the door open and stepped aside to let her in to the dimly lit shop. "Sorry about that. Every time there's a murder, Teresa starts locking the door as soon as it gets dark."

Every time there's a murder. That's something she never expected anyone in Crystal Shores to say. And every time there was a murder, she somehow happened to be there. It was starting to become disturbing to say the least.

Max felt something brush against her leg. "Oh, hello Josie," she said, as the black cat slipped in past her.

"There you are, you little stinker," Fiona said, scooping up the cat with one hand and closing the front door with the other. She led Max past wooden cubbies stuffed with balls of yarn and displays of beautifully knitted and crocheted scarves and sweaters.

She followed Fiona through the swinging doors into the back room.

"Sorry to not greet you properly at the front door," Teresa said, holding a skein of yarn between two hands. "You found Josie! Where was she hiding?"

"She wasn't hiding. She got out again." Fiona sat down, slipped on her reading glasses, and picked up the ball of yarn and continued to wind it from the skein Teresa was holding. "I have no idea how, but I'll figure it out one of these days."

"Looks like you're starting a new project," Max said with a smile.

Fiona peered at her over the rim of her reading glasses. "There's always a new project, dear. The day we don't have a new project is the day you better start planning our funerals."

"That's right," Teresa agreed. "We've started experimenting with some of the new trends. Keiko says young people are getting interested in knitting."

Max thought about the hipsters wearing knit caps even in warm Southern California, and she wasn't surprised. "Speaking of Keiko, I thought she would be here by now."

As if on cue, the door swung open and Keiko appeared wearing wide-legged black and white striped pants, a yellow t-shirt, and a black moto jacket covered in zippers. She held a takeout bag from House of Pies.

"Don't you look lovely," Teresa said. "And very on trend. I hope that jacket is vegan."

"I don't get it," Fiona butted in before Keiko could answer. "If someone is going to eat the cow, isn't it best to re-purpose the hide as an article of clothing?"

"Re-purpose?" Teresa seemed confused.

"Think about it. The first purpose is for the cow to wear, so it would be re-purposing to make it into a jacket." Fiona seemed to think that settled the matter. She turned back to Keiko. "Sit down, dear and let's see what you've brought us before we start talking about murder and suspects and such."

Keiko set the bag on the table and pulled out a box. While she opened it, she explained about the pies she had to choose from because, "After all, at this time of the day all the best pies are sold out. I got the last banana cream pie."

"Excellent choice," Fiona said, taking the box from Keiko.

"I never understood," Max said, "if they always sell out of the best ones then why don't they make more of them?"

Keiko looked at her and tilted her head. "Then, how would you know which ones are the best?"

Max opened her mouth to reply but thought better with arguing with Keiko logic, especially when she saw the sisters nodding in agreement.

Fiona retrieved plates and forks and began serving pie.

"But I haven't eaten dinner yet," Max protested.

Fiona shook her head slowly, muttering, "Young people."

"Life is short, Max," Teresa said. "You might as well eat dessert first."

As they dug into their oversized slices of rich, creamy pie, Keiko commented, "Bananas have lots of potassium."

The others contributed additional information on the many health benefits of banana cream pie until their plates were clean.

"Now can we talk about Xavier's murder?" Max asked. "I'm really worried about my dad. He doesn't have an alibi for the time of Xavier's murder."

"Plus, he's in love with Eliana," Keiko added.

"What?" Fiona and Teresa said at once.

"I was going to leave that part out," Max said. "I don't think it's relevant."

"No, no, no," Keiko protested. "If we're going to help you figure this out, you can't leave anything out. Even if you think it is not important. Agreed?"

The three women waited for her answer, so she finally gave in. "Agreed."

She filled Fiona and Teresa in on the details and what she had learned, including the witness who claimed to have seen Richard entering the office ten minutes sooner than he actually did. "Okay," Fiona chimed in when Max had finished updating them. "The murderer has to be Eliana, Henry, or the mysterious man in the fedora your father saw."

"Or Eliana or Henry are the mystery man in the fedora," Keiko said.

"Right," Fiona said.

"Or Leo," Max said. Everyone turned to stare at her. "What?"

"Leo's dead," Teresa said.

"Isn't he?" Fiona said.

Max shrugged. "Probably. I had a theory that he faked his death, but everyone seems to think that that's a crazy idea."

"I love crazy ideas," Fiona said. "Tell us more."

CHAPTER 18

*M*ax's father's house was dark, and his car wasn't parked in its usual spot in front. She really wanted to talk with him, but she supposed it would have to wait. She guessed he was at Eliana's again.

Sirens began to wail in the distance, and she listened as they grew louder and louder before stopping. They couldn't be more than a few blocks away.

She headed toward the ocean in the direction the sound had come from. It was probably a kitchen fire or an elderly neighbor afraid they were having a heart attack, but she needed to be sure her father was okay.

At the corner, she turned and saw flashing lights a few blocks away at what looked to be Eliana's street. She hurried down the sidewalk until she saw an ambulance, two police cars, and her father's Mini Cooper in front of Eliana's house.

A crowd had gathered on the sidewalk, and when she pushed through them, a uniformed officer stopped her.

"It's okay," a familiar voice called out. Of course, Jason was there.

Max rushed to him as he stepped onto the porch, closing the front door behind him. "Where's my dad? Is he okay? What's going on?"

"He's fine." Jason smiled as if to reassure her. "Calm down. Breathe."

"I'll breathe as soon as I find out what the heck is going on here."

"Not much, really. Eliana reported an intruder, but by the time we got here, he'd got away. She called Richard, and he wisely insisted that she call the police. I got here at the same time he did."

"And the ambulance?"

"Yeah. That was a bit of overkill. One of the newer dispatchers took the call, and we're just lucky he didn't call out the cavalry."

"I always liked living in a place where everyone overreacts because nothing ever happened here," Max said. "Maybe now it can get back to being a sleepy town where the biggest crime is jaywalking." She liked it that way, but did a detective get bored having so little crime to investigate? Was that why Jason was thinking of leaving?

They stood on the porch as if both wanted to say something, but before they did, Richard opened the door.

"Max," Richard said with surprise. "What are you doing here?"

"Something about flashing lights and your car parked nearby that caught my eye."

His eyes narrowed. "While you just happened to be walking by?"

"While I just happened to hear sirens and followed the sound. Why are you questioning me?"

Eliana appeared behind him. "Are you going to invite her in or just stand on the porch all evening?"

Max didn't wait for his reply, instead following Eliana into the living room, which was austerely decorated in neutral colors, not what she expected for the home of an artist. There wasn't a single painting on the walls. "I heard you had an attempted break in."

"More like a peeping Tom," Richard said. "Eliana saw someone looking in the window."

"I told you someone was following me," Eliana said to Richard. "Whoever killed Leo is coming after me. Now do you believe me?"

And people said Max had crazy theories. She sat down across from Richard and Eliana. "Who do you think is following you?"

Eliana glared at her. "How would I know? When I come home at night, I can tell someone is watching me. I get this feeling."

"A feeling?"

"I see. You don't believe me, either." Eliana stood up and walked out of the room, leaving Richard giving Max a scolding look.

Max followed Eliana into the kitchen and waited for her to pour herself a glass of wine. "You think someone killed Leo?"

Eliana took several gulps of wine before answering. She was obviously shaken up. "He was a skilled pilot. He had his plane checked regularly, and then he'd check it himself. He never took risks. If the weather wasn't perfect for flying, he didn't take off. I've never known anyone more cautious and calculating."

"But accidents do happen," Max said.

"And then," she continued, her voice steadier, "when I got back to town, the place had been searched."

"Someone ransacked your home?"

"No. It wasn't ransacked, but I could tell someone had been here. Little things were out of place." She excused herself and went upstairs.

Max returned to the living room. "It's not much to go on," she whispered to her dad.

"She's really afraid that someone is after her," he said. "She jumps at every sound. I'm worried about her. What if she's right?"

Max woke up the next morning to the sound of rain. She pulled the covers up to her chin and waited as long as possible to get out of bed. When she finally faced the day, her father offered her his car, so she wouldn't have to walk to work dodging puddles. She parked the Mini Cooper behind the shop and entered through the back door where the whirring of the sewing machine greeted her. Garrett stopped sewing and handed her a plastic container.

"My wife sent me with a carrot muffin for you plus some brownies just in case you don't like carrot muffins," he said, handing her the container.

Max peeked under the lid and the aroma was heavenly. "You don't have to bring me food or drink every day, you know. You're already on my good side."

"Do you have a bad side?" he asked but didn't wait for an answer. "My wife just wanted to express her appreciation for getting me out of the house every morning. I didn't realize how much I was annoying her moping around with nothing to do."

Max chuckled. "My dad was always sent to his studio after breakfast and not allowed back in the kitchen until lunchtime."

"Sounds like your mother and my wife are on the same page."

Max didn't want to spoil the cheerful moment by telling him her mother had passed away, so instead she said, "Your wife sounds like a lovely woman."

Garrett grinned. "She's the best." He showed Max the timer he'd brought. "Once an hour, I'll take a five-minute break."

"Sounds perfect. Do you want to split this muffin?" She asked.

"I had one for breakfast, but I'll take one of those brownies if you promise not to tell my wife," he said. "By the way, have you thought about what we talked about?"

"Oh. I really haven't had a chance to think. But I've always wanted to have my own fashion line. I love the shop, and I enjoy working with brides, but designing is my real love."

"Besides, if you were a designer, you could live anywhere. If you ever wanted to move, that is."

"I hadn't thought of that." Max wondered how much he knew about her relationship with Jason.

"As you said, you really haven't had a chance to think," he said.

"No, but I'll be doing a lot of thinking now."

Just before noon, the door jingled, announcing Heidi's arrival. Max waited for her to get settled, then asked her to watch the shop while she ran an errand. It was time to start asking questions.

#

THE SKIES HAD CLEARED, AND MAX DROVE SOUTH PAST the end of town where she had a view on her right of the ocean sparkling in the bright sun. When she reached Laguna Beach, she found a spot right in front of the Hildalgo Gallery.

The gallery looked different in the daylight. It had an abandoned feel to it, and no lights visible from outside. Max peered through the glass front door. Her father's paintings were still hung on the wall, but she didn't see any signs of life. Half expecting it to be closed, she was surprised when she found the door open.

She stepped inside and called out. "Hello? Anyone home?"

An elegant woman with short, dark hair appeared from behind a partition. Max recognized Xavier's assistant.

"May I help you?" Andrea said in a haughty voice. "Oh, it's you." She relaxed and smiled. "Sorry, the clients expect that snooty attitude from us."

"Really?" It occurred to Max that Andrea might have been close to her boss. "I'm sorry about Xavier."

"Thank you," Andrea said. "It was quite a shock. It's not like we were close, but I almost miss him bossing me around."

Max wanted to know more but remembered why she was there. "I'm looking for Henry. Is he around?

Andrea rolled her eyes. "He was supposed to be here two hours ago. We need to inventory everything and figure out the accounts. The phones have been ringing off the wall with artists wanting to know when they can pick up their artwork, but Henry keeps telling me he'll take care of it."

A phone in the back of the gallery rang.

"See what I mean?"

Max followed her into the main room past more of her father's paintings. She felt frumpy compared to Andrea in her black sheath and high-heeled strappy sandals. Max could barely walk in heels, but this woman made it appear effortless.

Andrea reached for the phone, which sat on top of

the tall reception desk, but it had already stopped ringing.

"Why do the artists want their artwork back?" Max asked. "Won't Henry be taking over the gallery?"

She huffed. "That's what Henry thinks, but he's in for a rude awakening. It's the owners who make a gallery successful, and it takes years to build up a reputation and clientele. If all the artists pull out, then what is he going to do with an empty gallery?"

"I get your point," Max said.

"Anyway, I don't think the gallery business is quite what Henry thought it would be. I think he only worked for his father because he thought he would be able to show his artwork." Andrea made air quotes when she said "artwork."

"Sounds like you're not that impressed with Henry's type of art," Max said.

Andrea leaned over the desk conspiratorially. "It was a thing a few years ago. Artist would find some interesting items at the junkyard or in a dumpster, put it on a pedestal and call it art. Let's just say I wasn't impressed with Henry's creations. Besides, found art is so last decade."

"It is?" Max was a bit embarrassed by how little she knew about the art world considering her father was an artist.

She twisted a strand of perfectly curled hair around one finger nervously. "I guess I shouldn't talk about my new boss like that, even if it is temporary."

"You must have gotten to know Xavier working for him. Do you have any theories about who killed him?"

Andrea shook her head. "No idea."

"He didn't have any enemies?" Max asked, disappointed.

"He had plenty of enemies," Andrea said with a wry smile. "Between the artists that weren't getting paid and the collectors asking for their deposits back, that would be a long list."

"He didn't pay the artists?"

"He'd pay them just enough to get them off his back," Andrea said. "I knew it would catch up with him eventually."

"Anyone seem particularly angry?" Max expected her to mention Eliana, since she must have known about their argument the night of the murder.

Andrea took a moment to reply. "Leo."

"Leo Baldassari?"

"If he were still alive, I'd have thought he did it. Leo and Xavier had a huge argument a few days before Leo's plane went down."

"What about?" Max prompted.

"Leo wanted to pick up all his paintings and Xavier refused at first. He said they had a contract and Leo couldn't show them at another gallery until the contract expired."

"What did Leo say about that?"

"He wouldn't take no for an answer," Andrea said. "He left with most of his paintings that afternoon. Xavier was in a foul mood the rest of the day."

"Interesting." Xavier wasn't lying when he told Eliana that Leo had picked up his paintings.

"But, since Leo is dead, I would guess it was one of the artists, or an angry collector perhaps. I suggested the idea to Henry."

"What did he say?"

Andrea turned her head at the sound of the front door. "He told me to mind my own business."

Max jumped when Henry came around the corner. He didn't look happy, but then he'd just lost his father.

"Hi, Henry," Max said.

"Hi." He paused for a moment. "I'm sorry, you're one up on me. I don't remember your name."

"I'm Max. Richard Walter's daughter. I'm so sorry for your loss. I lost my mother four years ago, and I have some idea of what you must be going through."

"Is that so?" He scowled. "Was your mother murdered, too?"

"Um, no." This was turning out to be really awkward.

"Exactly. So, unless you are here to tell me your father is turning himself in for my father's murder, I'd like you to leave."

"My dad didn't kill Xavier." There was no point in arguing with him especially when he'd just lost his father. "I shouldn't have stopped by," she said. "I apologize."

Henry turned and walked toward the back of the gallery without another word.

Max turned to Andrea. "I'll let myself out."

"If your dad knows any other galleries that might be hiring, let me know, okay?"

"Will do."

BACK IN THE CAR, SHE CONSIDERED STOPPING TO PICK UP a sandwich for lunch, but that would be cutting it too close if she wanted to be on time for her one-thirty appointment. She wouldn't suffer too much, though, since she had one of Garrett's wife's brownies left.

She checked in with Heidi and inspected the work Garrett had done so far, and it was impeccable. She would have to ask him how he managed to sew set-in sleeves without a single pucker. She rarely managed it herself.

Heidi helped her with her afternoon appointment, and for once, the bride knew what she wanted, and her maid of honor was cooperative and agreeable. Half an hour later Max was taking measurements so that she could order the right size. It all was going so smoothly. She should have known it wouldn't last.

"I'd like you to order the next size down," the bride said. "I've already lost ten pounds and I'm planning to lose at least twenty more before the wedding."

"Are you sure?" Max had heard this before, and in her experience, brides rarely lost weight before the wedding, no matter how good their intentions were.

The bride insisted, and her friend added her assurances.

Max gave it one more try. "You know these next

several months are going to be very stressful. Between working full time and planning your wedding, are you sure this is the best time for a diet? Personally, I think you look beautiful just the way you are."

That got a little smile from the bride, but it didn't change her decision.

When they left, Heidi asked, "Why didn't you want to order a smaller size if that's what she wants?"

"It is ten times easier to take in a dress than to let one out," Max explained. "And it's a hundred times more depressing for a bride when she can't fit in the dress she ordered. She feels like a failure at what is supposed to be a happy time."

"I hadn't thought of that," Heidi said. "What are you going to do?"

"I'm going to do what she requested." Max looked at her notes. "According to these measurements, she's a size fourteen."

"No," Heidi said, looking over her shoulder. "She's a twelve."

Max raised her eyebrows, hoping that Heidi would get the point. "Like I said, she's a size fourteen. So, I'll order her a size smaller, size twelve. Just like she asked me to."

Heidi frowned for a moment while she thought this over. Finally, she seemed to understand. "But what if she loses twenty pounds and the dress is too big?"

Max grinned. "If she loses twenty pounds, she'll be thrilled if the dress is too big, and I'll take it in for her. But if she doesn't, she'll still be able to fit into it."

"There's a lot more to being a bridal consultant than I thought," Heidi said. "I'll start putting the gowns away, so I can help you get ready for our next appointment."

CHAPTER 19

At six o'clock, Max locked the door behind Heidi, and as she reached up to pull down the blinds, she saw Keiko's face through the window. She unlocked the door and let her in.

"You're not answering your texts again," Keiko complained.

Max watched Keiko throw her messenger bag on one of the overstuffed chairs and throw herself onto another. "You know I don't check my phone when I'm working. You could have called if it was important." The moment she said it, it occurred to her that Keiko never called, only texted. "Did you need something?"

"Do you want to grab some dinner?" Keiko asked. "I forgot to eat lunch."

Max chuckled. "That's something you won't hear me saying, though come to think of it, I only had a brownie for lunch today. I need to work late, but we could order a pizza."

"Never mind," Keiko said. "I'll get something on the way home. I just wanted to run something by you. It's about Leo."

"Is it about the plane crash?"

"Not exactly. I've been thinking about the sculptures. You know how Simon and Teresa said he bought a Baldassari that looked just like the Bennett Landis sculpture that was at the gallery that night?"

"Yes," Max said. "That did seem odd."

"It seems a number of sculptures very similar to that style have suddenly been cropping up. It's quite a coincidence that no one had ever heard of Bennett Landis before Leo's plane went down, don't you think?"

Too much of a coincidence as far as Max was concerned. "What do you think it means? Is this guy copying Leo's style and trying to profit from his death?"

"That doesn't make sense," Keiko said. "If someone wanted to copy his style and capitalize on his death, it would be smarter to copy his paintings. You know, become the next 'Painter of Brilliance'."

"Okay, I don't' get it," Max said. "You already said it was way too hard to fake your own death."

"I know what I said. I'm starting to think he may have pulled it off."

"He is alive!" Max exclaimed with a fist pump. "Knew it!"

Keiko raised one eyebrow. "It's a bit early to gloat."

"He's alive, he's alive," Max sang happily, doing a little dance.

"I don't know why you're happy," Keiko said. "If he is alive, which is still just a theory, it complicates things."

Max grinned. "Unless he's the one who knocked Xavier over the head with a bust."

Keiko thought about this. "I guess you're right. That would actually simplify things. But why would Leo want to kill Xavier?"

"Xavier must have been in on the scam," Max said.

"What scam?" Keiko asked.

"Think about it. Leo would need someone to promote him as a promising yet reclusive new sculptor."

"You might be on to something," Keiko said. "But then why kill Xavier?"

Max had given this question some thought. "If Xavier was the only person who knew Leo was alive, maybe he decided to blackmail him. He wouldn't be the first person to die because he got greedy."

"If he is alive, and remember, it is a big if, do you think Eliana knows?" Keiko asked. "They might have dreamed up this scheme together, don't you think?"

"If she knew Leo was alive," Max said, "then she would have known he had picked up his paintings from the gallery. Besides, she's convinced his death was suspicious, and he's too good of a pilot and too careful to crash his plane in perfect weather conditions."

"When were you going to tell me that?" Keiko asked.

"As soon as I remembered to tell you," Max said. "Which I just did."

Keiko stood, picked up her messenger bag, and walked toward the door to leave. When she reached the door, she turned back and said, "Don't do anything crazy without talking to me first." Then she was gone.

Max stared at the door as it swung shut. "Me?" she said to herself. "It's like she doesn't even know me sometimes."

Max was in the middle of cutting out the lining for Daphne's gown when Richard called to see when she would be home with his car. She had completely forgotten that she had driven it to work that day.

On the short drive home, she made a decision. Her father needed to know. If Leo was alive, that meant Eliana was a married woman, not a widow. The longer before Richard found out, the more it would hurt.

She parked in front of the house and went through the front gate instead of around the back. The lights were on, but the front door was locked, which wasn't typical. She knocked.

A few moments later, Richard swung open the door. Max got a whiff of aftershave as she entered the living room. He wore dress slacks and a black V-neck sweater. Obviously, he had a date, and she could guess who it was with.

"Nice sweater. I don't remember seeing it before," Max remarked casually as she followed him into the kitchen. "Are you going out to eat?"

"Eliana is making me dinner." He pulled out a bottle of wine from the refrigerator. "It's been a long time since I had a home cooked meal."

"What are you talking about? You cook all the time."

Richard chuckled. "It's not exactly the same when you have to do all the work."

"I do the dishes," Max said. "Well, most of the time, anyway."

"Thanks for bringing the car home. It's close enough to walk, but the weather report says we'll be getting some more rain this evening."

"Dad," Max began, "can I talk to you for a minute?"

Richard pulled on his jacket. "Now?"

"Yes. I need to talk to you about Eliana."

Richard took a deep breath as if to calm himself before answering. "Max, I don't know why you don't like her. She's a lovely lady, and I plan to see a lot more of her."

"Dad, it doesn't matter if I like her or not," she began.

"True, but I do wish—"

"There's something you need to know," Max interrupted him. "I think Leo is alive. If he is, then that means Eliana isn't a widow."

"Max, that's crazy," Richard said. "Why would you make up a story like that? Does it bug you so much to see me with someone other than your mother?"

"It's not that—"

"I loved your mother. I loved her with all my heart and planned to spend all my life with her. But it didn't work out that way. For a long time, I didn't think I'd ever be happy again. But I am, Max. I'm happy. I wish you could be happy for me."

"I want you to be happy. You know I do. But Dad, if Leo is alive, don't you want to know?"

Richard reached out his hands. "Keys, please."

Max reached into her purse and dug around for the car keys. "Please don't say anything to Eliana. Not until we have proof."

"Don't worry, I won't." He snatched the keys from her hand. "You'd better get used to the idea of me being with Eliana. And if you can't accept her, then it might be time for you to find another place to live." He walked out the front door and let it slam shut behind him.

Max stood in the living room trying to remember how to breathe. It had never occurred to her that he would take Eliana's side over hers, and even kick her out of her apartment. She felt a tear roll down her cheek and wiped it away with the back of her hand.

She hadn't felt so alone since the day her mother had died. Had she lost her father now, too? She'd always known her father might get married again, but she never thought that a woman would come between them.

CHAPTER 20

Max looked around her father's living room. Not much had changed since her mother had passed away, except for a few new paintings on the wall. The furniture, rugs, and the paint on the walls hadn't changed, but everything else had.

The phone rang, and she answered it as soon as she saw Jason's name on the display. "I wanted to talk to you before I left," he said.

"You're leaving?" Max forced her voice to sound calm. "To Miami?"

"Yes," he said. "My interview with the hiring committee is Thursday. My old chief says it's just a formality, really. He's already told me I have the job if I want it."

Max searched for the right words to say. She wanted to tell him not to go or to take her with him. Instead, she said, "Congratulations."

There was silence on the other end of the phone.

"Jason? Are you still there?"

"That's all you have to say?" he asked.

"I don't know what to say," Max said. "I don't want you to go, you know that, right?"

"Why did it take so long for you to say it?"

Good question. Why hadn't she begged him not to leave? "I'm not going to stand in the way of your career."

"But you're afraid to start a new life with me."

"Afraid?" Max's felt an immediate rush of anger, and she wondered if he heard it over the phone line.

"Bad choice of words," he said. "You have too much here to leave, I know. Look, I'll be back in a few days. We can talk then."

"Okay," Max said, and after hesitating a moment added, "I love you," before she realized he'd already ended the call.

Why didn't she tell him they could have a long-distance relationship until they figured it out? But could they? It seemed like they could only be together if one of them gave in and forgot about their own plans and dreams.

What Max wanted was Jason. She knew it in her heart, and she nearly picked up the phone to call him back. She stared at Jason's name displayed on the phone screen, but something kept her from making the call.

The doorbell brought her back to reality. She

looked around for a box of tissues and settled for wiping her tears away with a napkin. Whoever was at the door must have been impatient, since they knocked again. Another round of knocks, louder now, started before she reached the door.

She opened the door to discover the impatient visitor was Detective Gallagher. Great.

"I'm looking for Richard Walters." he said.

"Hello to you, too," Max replied, annoyed by his rudeness. "He's not in."

"I have called repeatedly and left several messages. Where is he?"

"He's out," Max said, just in case the detective didn't know what "he's not in" meant. She hoped he wouldn't ask any more questions, because she didn't want to have to lie. And she was not about to tell him anything unless she had to.

"Have him call me as soon as he returns," Gallagher demanded. "Tonight."

"Okay," Max said. "I'll leave him a note in case I don't see him."

"Make sure he calls me."

"Why do you want to talk to him again?" Max asked. "You've interviewed him twice. What else do you need to know?"

"I don't share the details of my investigations with civilians."

Max wanted badly to tell him off, but instead she said, "Leo might still be alive." When she saw his blank look, she continued. "Leo Baldassari, the artist? He might be the killer."

Gallagher's face turned pink on its way to red. "Stay out of the investigation. Do you hear me? I am perfectly willing to throw you in jail for obstruction of justice." He barreled his way back to the front patio door, pausing once to turn and glare at her. In response, she slammed the door. Hard.

Max left a note for her father on his bed, assuming he would be sleeping at home. He seemed to have it bad for Eliana, and Max hoped he wouldn't be hurt too badly when he found out the truth, whatever that was.

She still had work to do at the shop and would rather work than stay at home and mope, but she wasn't about to skip dinner. She called Angelo's and ordered a small pepperoni pizza to pick up on the way.

The crescent moon didn't provide much light as she walked down Rose Street to the restaurant. Only the main streets had streetlights, and the darkness never bothered her before, but now every shadow seemed to hide someone or something ready to pounce. She heard a sound behind her. It sounded like footsteps, but when she turned around the footsteps stopped and there was no one there. No one she could see at any rate.

"Now I'm the one getting paranoid," she muttered to herself.

The traffic and bright lights on Coast Highway reassured her and by the time she picked up her pizza, she chastised herself for being afraid of the dark.

A few very productive hours of sewing later as she was putting her supplies away; she heard a noise at the door. Her heart pounded in her chest as she turned every light on in the showroom. She cautiously approached the front door and peeked through the blinds. No one was there.

CHAPTER 21

A loud wail made her jump out of her skin, and she looked down to see a black cat sitting outside of the door. She opened it, and Josie waltzed in as if she owned the place.

"Josie, what are you doing out?" she asked the cat, but Josie gave no answer, just jumped up on one of the easy chairs, curled up, and began to purr.

Max called Teresa to let her know where her cat was. "No, Josie's with Fiona," Teresa assured her. "Simon and I are in Big Bear."

"Are you saying I don't know your cat?"

There was silence on the line for several moments. "It really is her? That little rascal. She's been getting out a lot lately, but I don't see how she ended up at Wedding Belles. I'll call Fiona right now."

"Don't worry, I'll call her," Max said.

"That darn cat," Fiona said the moment she walked through the door. She addressed the cat directly. "I've had about enough of your shenanigans. You're just lucky that Max was working late. Why are you working late?"

Max realized that the last part of Fiona's rant was directed to her. "Catching up on one of my custom gowns. I have a fitting on Friday."

"You've been putting in a lot of hours lately. What does your boyfriend think about that?"

Max winced but brushed off the question. "He works a lot too, you know."

"And Richard? Isn't he lonely without you around?"

"Don't you worry about him," Max said with a note of sarcasm. "He's got Eliana to keep him company."

"I see," Fiona said. "You two are so close. I'm sure he misses spending time with you."

"No, I'm pretty sure he doesn't, and he's definitely not interested in what I have to say."

"Uh-huh. What did you say?" Fiona said as if she had a pretty good idea already.

Max didn't look at Fiona, having a strong feeling she was going to scold her. "Leo might be alive. He might be a murderer. I had to say something."

Fiona put a hand on Max's shoulder and gently maneuvered her onto the sofa and took a seat next to her. "You never, ever criticize someone else's love interest."

"You know he's in love with her?"

"Did you even hear the part about not criticizing her?"

Josie jumped up on the sofa next to Max and

climbed on her lap. After walking in a circle, she curled up and began purring loudly.

"But if Leo is alive, then my dad's dating a married woman," Max said, stroking Josie's sleek black fur. "He needed to know."

"Why? Is he in danger?"

"Maybe." The look on Fiona's face told her that she wasn't buying it. "I suppose not."

"When you criticize her, his instinct is to come to her defense. Instead of driving them apart, you've practically pushed him into her arms."

"I have?" Max hadn't considered that, but it made sense. When she was barely a teenager, there was a boy Max thought she liked but her mother told her not to see him. She kept seeing him long after she lost interest. She was as stubborn as her father. "What do I do now?"

"Apologize. The sooner the better."

Max made a face like she'd just tasted something gross.

"But don't make that face when you do it."

Max laughed. "Okay, how's this?" She plastered a big smile on her face.

Fiona didn't look convinced. "Maybe practice in front of a mirror."

"Okay. Thanks for the advice, Fiona."

"Thanks for keeping an eye on this little rascal." Fiona reached for Josie who didn't seem happy about being disturbed from her nap. "Let me know what happens, okay?"

"You got it."

After Fiona left, Max grabbed her purse and locked up the shop. No time like the present.

Max walked down the dark street, but when she reached her father's house, there wasn't a single light on. She stood on the sidewalk staring at the empty house wondering what she should do while she waited for her father to come home.

A walk always made her feel better and think more clearly. She began walking toward the ocean, and without meaning to, found herself heading toward Eliana's house.

Max barely heard the sound of the waves crashing and the barking sea lions while she walked along Ocean Avenue. Unlike the smaller side streets, here the streetlights lit up the sidewalk nearly as bright as day. Two locals walking their dogs passed her with a quick hello.

Richard's car was parked in front of Eliana's house, and Max stood on the sidewalk staring at the dark house. Why were there no lights on that she could see? Never mind. She didn't want to know.

She took a few steps toward the front door. Maybe they were on the back patio, if she had a back patio, or dining by candlelight. It wasn't that late, after all. She glanced at her phone, surprised to see it was almost eleven o'clock. She might as well go home and wait until tomorrow to apologize to her father.

Before she turned to leave, she heard voices inside the house. She stopped and listened as they got louder.

Were they having a fight? She stepped onto the patio and raised her hand to knock on the door.

Her father was yelling something, but she couldn't make out the words. Before she could decide what to do, she heard what sounded like a gunshot. And then a scream. A woman's scream.

Lights came on inside and Max banged on the door, no longer concerned about interrupting them. She had to make sure her dad was all right. When no one answered, she tried the door and was surprised when it opened.

She ran into the empty living room where two empty wine glasses sat on the coffee table. "Dad?" she called out. No answer.

She passed through the dining room and into the kitchen where she stopped, not understanding what she was seeing.

Eliana stood over a shaggy-haired, bearded man who lay motionless on the floor as her father looked on, appearing to be in a trance. In his hand was a gun.

"Dad," Max called out to him. He turned to her, and then stared at the gun in his hand. She grabbed a kitchen towel and took the gun from him, placing it on the counter.

Dialing 9-1-1 on her cell phone, she knelt down next to the stranger. She felt for a pulse, hoping it wasn't too late for the man on the floor, but she didn't feel even a flutter. "A man's been shot," she told the dispatcher and gave them the address.

She held the towel over the man's chest, hoping to

slow the bleeding, but with a sinking feeling inside. He'd been shot through the heart or close to it.

She looked up at her father. "What the heck happened?"

"He broke in," Richard began. "Eliana had a gun."

"Your father saved my life," Eliana said.

Max could hear the dispatcher on the phone trying to get her attention. "Hurry, please." she said, though she knew it was too late.

Eliana kept talking frantically. "I told you I was being followed, Richard. I told you someone was watching the house." She took a few steps toward the man on the floor, stopped, and began to shriek. "It's Leo! It's Leo!"

Max watched her father pull Eliana away from the body and wrap her in his arms. Leo had been alive after all, just as Max had suspected. Only now he was dead.

Sirens sounded in the distance, and Eliana continued to sob. She pulled away from Richard, turned, and ran up the stairs.

Max tried to make sense of everything but failed. "Dad," she asked. "What happened?"

"Eliana heard a noise. Said someone was trying to get in. I didn't see her get the gun—I just followed her downstairs. There was a man, that man, and Eliana was pointing a gun at him. I tried to take the gun from her, but it went off." He looked at the man lying on the floor. "Is that really Leo?"

Max still held the towel pressed against his chest,

knowing it was pointless. "It must be, if Eliana says it is."

The paramedics arrived and confirmed what Max had suspected. Leo Baldassari was dead. Max called Jason, but the call went to voice mail.

"I don't understand," Richard said. "How could it be Leo? He's been dead four months."

"Dad." She wanted to understand what had happened before the police arrived. "When Eliana heard the noise, you were both upstairs?" At least her father was fully clothed. It would have been even more awkward if he'd been wearing a robe or Leo's old pajamas.

"It's not what you think," Richard said. "Eliana was convinced someone has been following her and might try to break into the house again. I was going to sleep in the spare bedroom, just so she could feel safer. I'll be honest, I thought she was imagining being followed and hearing noises."

Max had so many questions. "Why would he break in?"

Eliana appeared at the bottom of the stairs. "I wish I knew the answer to that question. I thought my husband was dead."

There was coldness in Eliana's eyes. "How could he do that to me?" Max knew she didn't expect an answer. "I knew someone was following me. I just never dreamed it was Leo."

"What was he doing here?" He must have been after

something in the house. "Was he looking for something?"

Eliana shook her head. "There was something familiar about him, even in the dark," she said, in a faraway voice. "It was the way he moved. If only—" She blinked back tears, though Max didn't know if they were tears of sadness, regret, or anger.

If Eliana was telling the truth, she'd been through a grueling ordeal, losing her husband twice, the second time by killing him herself. But if she were lying, well, then Eliana was a cold-blooded murderer.

And her father was in love with her.

WHEN THE CRYSTAL SHORES POLICE ARRIVED, AN OLDER detective arrived followed by two officers in a patrol car. The detective questioned Max briefly, but when he learned that Max hadn't been in the house at the time of the shooting, he told her she could go home. He asked Eliana and Richard to accompany him to the police station.

Richard tossed Max his car keys. "I'll see you in the morning," he said. "You don't need to wait up for me."

Max couldn't read the look on his face, but he must have been filled with a number of conflicting emotions. He'd been so angry with her, and it turned out she'd been right about Leo.

Max followed everyone outside and watched her father and Eliana being put in the back of two different police cars. Max guessed they didn't want them talking to each other until they got their statements.

Neighbors stood on the sidewalk, and she looked around at the crowd to see if she recognized anyone. She pressed the remote for the Mini Cooper and it beeped cheerfully, as if everything were perfectly normal.

When she reached the car, Jason stepped forward and opened her door.

"What took you so long?" she asked.

"I was on the way when I got a call from the police chief. When he found out you were at the scene, he put another detective on the case."

"Then why are you here?" she asked.

"I came to make sure you were okay." He looked over his shoulder as if to see if anyone was listening. "Why don't we talk in the car?"

Max sat in the driver's seat and waited for Jason to come around the other side. As soon as he opened the door, she began talking. "The gun went off when my dad tried to grab it from her. I think he was shot right in the heart."

"What were you doing at Eliana's house anyway?" he asked.

"I came by to apologize to my dad. We'd had a fight earlier. About Eliana. But I couldn't see any lights on in the house, so I was going to go home when I heard a gunshot. I went in and found Leo on the floor."

"So, Leo was shot in the dark?"

Max thought about what he'd said. "No wonder she

didn't recognize him." She leaned back against the headrest and stared at the crowd still gathered. "I hope they don't arrest my dad."

"Worst-case scenario, it would be manslaughter," Jason said.

"Manslaughter!" Max sat up straight. "You think they're going to arrest my dad for manslaughter?"

"No, of course not." Jason reached over the gearshift, took her hand, and squeezed it gently. "They're just questioning him. It's routine."

"He can't claim self-defense when the victim didn't have a weapon."

"Max, you're getting ahead of yourself."

Max looked down at his hand wrapped around hers. Somehow it wasn't as comforting as she would have expected.

"Do you want me to stay with you?" he asked.

Max closed her eyes and longed to feel his strong arms around her and hear him tell her everything would be okay. But it wasn't okay. "No. I appreciate it, but you have a plane to catch in the morning, don't you?"

"That's right. I'd almost forgotten. That doesn't mean I wouldn't stay if you wanted company."

"I'll be fine," she said, and started the car.

Jason opened the car door and stepped out. "Call me if you need me," he said, shutting the door before she had a chance to respond.

"If I need you," Max said quietly to herself, "you'll be in Miami."

CHAPTER 22

$\mathcal{M}$ax made a pot of tea, curled up on the sofa in her dad's living room, and waited for word from him. She didn't care if he said not to wait up. She'd stay up all night just to know he was okay. The clock slowly ticked away the minutes, and the sound begin to lull her to sleep.

Sometime after midnight, she awoke with a start when the front door opened. Her dad was home, and she jumped off the sofa and threw her arms around him.

"I thought I told you not to wait up," he said with a chuckle. "Do you ever listen to me?"

"Of course," Max said, "but I was worried about you. What happened at the police station?"

"Eliana and I gave our statements, and they let us go home. Now why don't you get some sleep," he suggested.

"So, they're not going to arrest you?" she asked.

"You have such a vivid imagination. It's one of the things I love about you, but sometimes you get a bit carried away." He sat down next to her. "Except that sometimes you're right. I'm sorry I didn't believe you about Leo."

"That's okay." She leaned her head on his shoulder and felt ten years old again. "It must have sounded like another of my crazy theories."

"It sure did."

She held back tears. "I love you."

"Love you, too, Sunshine," he said wearily.

She wanted nothing more than to break down in tears of relief, but she took a deep breath and headed to her little apartment, where she made herself a cup of hot cocoa and curled up on her sofa. With all the excitement, she knew she wouldn't be able to fall asleep for hours.

MAX WOKE UP WHEN SHE HEARD HER PHONE BUZZING. She turned over to reach for it and fell off the sofa.

"Ouch!" She rubbed her knee. That was going to leave a bruise. She'd fallen asleep in an awkward position and stretched her stiff neck to get the kink out. It took her a moment to remember why she was sleeping in the living room in her clothes.

At least the phone had stopped buzzing. She picked it up and saw a message from Garrett. *Where r u?*

She squinted at the phone. Ten thirty? She texted back: *On my way.*

There was no time for a shower, coffee, or anything else. Hopefully no one would notice she was wearing the same clothes from yesterday, but if they did, she didn't care.

She ducked into the bathroom to wipe the mascara off from under her eyes and brush her teeth before grabbing her purse and jacket.

Running down the stairs, she saw the curtains were open in her father's kitchen window. She opened the back door and found him sitting at the table.

Richard looked up when she entered. "Aren't you supposed to be at work?"

"I overslept. Can we talk tonight?"

"Sure. Hold on a second." He stood up from the table.

"Really gotta run, Dad." Max followed him into the living room.

Richard tossed her his car keys. "Might as well get there a few minutes sooner."

"Thanks, Dad. You're the best." Max pulled open the front door and jumped back when she saw Detective Gallagher and two uniformed officers coming straight toward her.

"What do you want?" Max said. She was in no mood for Gallagher's attitude this morning.

"Where is Richard Walters?" Gallagher asked with a scowl on his bulldog face.

"Why?" she asked. "What do you want?"

Richard appeared at her side. "It's alright, Max. I can handle this. You go to work."

Max gave her father another hug and stepped past the detective and the officers. Before she reached the patio gate, she heard Gallagher's booming voice.

"Richard Walters, you're under arrest for the murder of Xavier Hidalgo."

"What?" Max hurried back to her father's side. "You can't arrest him. What proof do you have?"

"You'll find out soon enough," Gallagher said while one of the officers pulled out his handcuffs.

"Is this really necessary?" Richard asked Gallagher, who seemed to consider the question.

"Fine." He nodded to the officer who put the cuffs away.

"Max, call my lawyer." Richard said. "He'll know what to do."

"But, Dad," Max began to protest.

"Just do it," Richard said, and turned back to the officer. "Let's go."

Max ran back inside, found the attorney's number, and had him on the phone in minutes. He told her not to worry, that he had an associate who was an excellent defense attorney.

"As soon as I get in touch with him, I'll head over to the police station myself and see if Richard needs anything."

"Thank you." Max blinked back tears. "And call me as soon as you know something."

She looked down at her hand, which still clutched her father's keys. There was nothing else she could do from home, and she still had responsibilities.

When the car turned the corner onto Coast Highway, she could see someone waiting in front of her shop. Her first appointment, no doubt, though she wondered why she wasn't waiting inside. From a block away, she could see the woman was fuming.

As she got closer, the client waited impatiently for Max to park the car in front of the shop. "I've been waiting over half an hour," she huffed. "How can you run a business with such poor customer service? The man inside wouldn't even let me come in and sit down. He was terribly rude. But I suppose that's what you get when you hire just anyone to work for you."

"Excuse me?" Max hoped she didn't mean what it sounded like.

"I expect an apology. I rearranged my schedule especially for this appointment, which wasn't easy, let me tell you. My time is valuable, you know."

"Of course, your time is valuable. I apologize. Something very serious came up and I wasn't able to get here sooner."

"I see. I suppose I should have expected an excuse from you. My mother told me to go to Allure Bridal. I should have listened to her."

"Yes, perhaps you should have," Max replied wearily.

"What?" The woman put her hands on her hips. "How dare you speak to a customer like that?"

"You're no longer a customer," Max said. "I've already apologized. Would you like me to get you the number for Allure Bridal so you can make an appointment with them?" Max stepped past her to unlock the front door.

"I'm going online right now and give you a one-star review," was the last thing Max heard before she shut the door and locked it behind her.

Garrett emerged from the workroom. "I'm sorry Max. I know I should have let her in, but I didn't like her attitude."

"I didn't like it either," Max said, throwing herself onto one of the easy chairs. A knock on the door startled her, and she looked up to see Heidi peering in.

"I'll let her in," Garrett said.

Heidi was in a fluster. "Why is the door locked? Did you forget to unlock it?"

"No," Max said, "I didn't forget. We're not opening today. I need you to call all of our appointments for today and tomorrow and reschedule them." When Heidi hesitated, she added, "Please?"

"Are you okay?" Heidi asked. "Is the business closing? I thought it was doing well. Do I need to find another job?"

Max closed her eyes for a moment. When she reopened them, she said, "The business is fine. Would you please call the appointments?"

"Jeez," Heidi muttered and shuffled off to the office. "I was just asking."

Max's phone rang, and she answered it on the first ring. The new attorney was on his way to the police station but had already called and spoken to an officer. Gallagher hadn't charged Richard and only had twenty-four hours to do so, or they had to release him.

"The officer I spoke with wasn't especially forthcoming," the lawyer said. "I will call you after I speak with your father and the detective on the case."

Garrett calmly listened to her side of the conversation, and when she hung up, he said, "What can I do to help?"

"Coffee?" she said with a weak smile.

"Coming right up," he said. "I've already made a pot of my special blend. Cream and sugar, correct?"

Max sighed gratefully. "That would be wonderful."

Garrett and Max took their coffee to the workroom. Max filled him in on the events of the previous evening and told him about Richard's arrest that morning between gulps of coffee. Garrett called his personal attorney who assured him that Richard had excellent representation.

"What do you usually do in this situation?" Garrett asked.

"I haven't been in this situation before. Having my father arrested for murder is a first for me."

"Yes, but solving a murder isn't."

Max regarded him in a new light. "You've heard."

"Your neighbor Fiona came over earlier looking for you. She heard about the shooting and wanted to check on you. You're lucky you have such loyal friends and family."

Max considered this with a pang of guilt. "Well, my dad's in jail and I think everyone else is mad at me."

"What are you talking about? I've never seen any group of people care about someone the way your friends care about you. And that's in spite of the fact that you have been putting work ahead of everything else. I know what I'm talking about."

"But you were so successful," Max said.

"Yes, and I almost lost everything I truly cared about. I ended up in the hospital with a triple bypass, but I wasn't going to let that slow me down. It wasn't until my wife threatened to leave me that I realized what I could lose. She was tired of being taken for granted."

Max grimaced. "I have been taking everyone for granted, haven't I? But how do I make it better? I don't want to be that person who only has time for my friends when I need something."

"You need to learn a lesson," he said, and left the workroom. She stood up and watched him walk right out the front door.

Great. Had she ticked off Garrett, too? She had no idea what she'd done to upset him. And he didn't even bring her a refill. She picked up her cup and went to the office for more coffee. Heidi sat hunched over the computer.

"How's it going, Heidi?" she asked, but didn't get an answer. "I'm sorry if I was short with you. There's a lot going on right now, but you're doing a great job and I want you to know how much I appreciate you."

"Really?" Heidi said in her little girl voice. "And the shop isn't going out of business?"

"Far from it," Max said. "I've got more work than I can handle, which is why I'm so grateful to have you and Keiko and Garrett."

Max heard the front door jingle and Fiona's voice calling, "Max? Where are you?"

Max walked into the showroom and saw that Garrett had returned with Fiona, who ran up to her and encompassed her in a tight hug. It was one of those hugs that lasts a really long time. When Fiona finally released her, Max said, "Thank you for coming."

"What are friends for?" Fiona said. "Garrett gave me a quick rundown, and it's time to get the team in action."

"The team?" At first, Max didn't know what Fiona was talking about, and then she smiled. She was part of a team, and had always been part of a team, even when she tried to shut everyone out and do everything herself.

"Keiko is meeting us next door," Fiona said, "and Teresa is already on her way. "

Max frowned. "Teresa is cutting back her vacation? I don't want her to do that."

"Pshaw and fiddlesticks." Fiona grinned. "Teresa and Simon headed home as soon as she heard that Richard had been arrested. Honestly, I think she was happy for the excuse to come home. It's cold and snowing up in Big Bear, and she says she'd seen enough snow to last a lifetime after spending so many winters in Canada. Besides, she misses everyone."

"You mean she misses Josie," Max said.

Garrett had been listening to the two women talk. "Who's Josie?"

"The cat," Fiona and Max said at once.

"Which reminds me," Fiona said. "I'd better get her before she sneaks out again. Shall we go?"

"Go?" Max asked.

"Yes," Fiona said. "You are distracted, dear, and no wonder. Keiko and Teresa are meeting us at our shop. I thought it would be quieter there." She turned to Garrett. "That is if you and Heidi will watch the shop for a bit."

"The door's locked and Heidi is here to answer the phone. Don't you worry about us," Garrett assured them.

"Thanks, Garrett," Max said. "Anything you need before I go?"

"We'll be fine," Garrett said. "You go and I'll keep an eye on things here."

CHAPTER 23

*M*ax followed Fiona next door and waited for her to unlock the front door. "Did anyone call Eric?" Max knew Eric would be terribly offended if he wasn't included.

"Yes, of course," Fiona said. "He said he had an errand to run, but he'll meet us shortly." She stepped inside her shop, turning on lights as she made her way to the back. "I figured we could talk more freely here with fewer ears to overhear us. Take a seat at the table, and I'll make a pot of coffee." She disappeared through the swinging doors that separated the back area.

Max pulled up a chair at the big oak table that took up half the room. It had been years since she'd sat at this table, and it brought back memories of when her mother had taken knitting lessons from the sisters. They called them lessons, but they could more accurately be described as social gatherings with a bit of coaching thrown in.

Before Fiona returned with coffee, Keiko burst in. "I'm here. Am I late?"

"You're right on time," Max said.

"The sign at Wedding Belles says closed." Keiko threw her messenger bag on a chair.

"We *are* closed. I have Heidi cancelling all our appointments for today and tomorrow."

"Good," Keiko said. "Where are Fiona and Teresa?"

Right on cue, Fiona entered from the back holding Josie in her arms. The cat wiggled to get free, until Fiona gave up trying to wrangle her and let her jump down to the floor.

"I'm keeping an eye on you today, young lady," Fiona scolded the cat.

"Have you figured out how she's getting out yet?" Max asked.

"Not exactly," Fiona said. "But we know she has an escape route out the back. Then she walks all the way down the alley to the side street and back around the front. The new people at the bakery were giving her treats until I asked them to stop, but now she just bothers random people on the street or scratches at other shop doors. She's a stinker, all right."

"How about we figure out Josie's escape route after we get my dad out of jail," Max suggested.

"Of course, dear," Fiona agreed. "Let me lock the front door, so we don't have any interruptions."

"But you're open today, aren't you?" Keiko asked.

"If anyone wants yarn, they can knock. We don't get

much business during the week anyway. Thanks to Keiko, our online orders keep us in business."

Before she reached the door, it swung open, and Eric entered with a huge box from a Newport Beach bakery. Everything Eric did was upscale and exclusive, even his pastries. Before Fiona could close the door behind him, her sister Teresa arrived.

"I'm back," Teresa said. "What have I missed?"

Teresa greeted Max and Keiko and admired the bakery box Eric had brought. "Ooh, fancy. I've been meaning to try Antoine's since they opened, but they're so expensive."

"Nothing is too good for my favorite murder ladies," Eric said.

Fiona gaped at him. "Murder ladies? Is that what you're calling us now?" She seemed to think this over for a moment, her brow knit in concentration, and then she grinned. "I think I like it."

While Fiona poured coffee and Eric passed around pastries, Max filled them in on Leo's death and Richard's arrest for Xavier's murder. After she finished, the questions began.

Fiona was first. "Why in the world do they think Richard could possibly murder anyone?"

"I'm waiting to hear more from the lawyer," Max said, "but I'm hoping Gallagher gets some sense soon and doesn't press charges."

"The very idea," Fiona said. "It's just too—"

"So, who pulled the trigger?" Eric asked.

"What?" Keiko turned and stared at Eric. "Xavier was hit over the head with a sculpture."

"Not Xavier," Eric said. "Leo."

"My dad reached for the gun to get it away from Eliana, and it went off," Max explained.

"The question is," Fiona said, "did Eliana fire the gun accidentally because your dad's hand was on hers, or did she fire it on purpose before he could take it away from her?"

Keiko nodded. "Who shoots someone through the heart on accident?"

"You were there right after the shooting," Teresa chimed in. "How did she act when she realized it was her husband?"

Max closed her eyes, recreating the scenario in her mind. When she opened them, she said, "She seemed genuinely shocked. And really, really angry."

"That's an interesting reaction," Eric said.

"But understandable," Keiko said. "Her husband faked his death. No doubt to cheat his creditors, the public, and especially his wife."

"I'd be angry enough to spit nails if my husband had faked his death and kept me in the dark about it," Fiona said. "And then to break into her house. Does anyone have any idea why he broke in?"

"No," Max said. "Eliana said she couldn't think of a reason. She seemed as perplexed as we were."

"I guess it's just another unsolved mystery," Eric said.

Max tried to put all the puzzle pieces together in

her head, but the clues refused to line up in an orderly fashion. "It must have been Leo who killed Xavier."

"Why?" Keiko asked. "Do you think that's who your dad saw go out the back door?"

"It makes sense, doesn't it?" She shared with the others her theory that Xavier knew Leo was alive and was helping him make a new start.

"Xavier might have been blackmailing Leo," Keiko said. "Or decided he didn't want to be part of his scam anymore. Leo might not have trusted him to keep quiet."

"That seems plausible," Eric said.

"More than plausible." Fiona stood up from the table. "I think we have our killer. How do we prove it, so we can get Richard off the hook?"

Max stared into the bottom of her empty coffee cup. When had she drunk it? She felt as if she were in a daze. "It all adds up," she told herself, not even realizing she spoke out loud.

Keiko cocked her head. "Then why don't you look convinced?"

"Have you ever done a jigsaw puzzle?" Max asked.

Keiko said, "No," at the same time the others said, "Yes."

Max turned to Fiona. "You know how sometimes, a piece seems to fit perfectly, only it's the wrong piece?"

"I hate that," Fiona agreed. "You can never finish the puzzle until you find that one piece."

Max nodded. "The one piece that is in the wrong

place. I keep feeling like someone is in the wrong place."

"What does that mean, Max?" Fiona asked.

"I wish I knew." Max stood up, impatient to do something other than just talk. "But the important thing is making sure my father doesn't get charged with murder. Leo is a much more likely murderer than my dad. Someone who would fake his own death might do just about anything."

"Okay, then. What's the plan?" Fiona asked.

"Do you think you and Teresa could go talk to Eliana?" Max asked. "See if she's figured out what Leo was looking for."

"You bet! We'll go to offer our condolences, now that her husband is dead again. I suppose it's a good thing she didn't know he was alive before she killed him."

Keiko raised her eyebrows. "A good thing?"

"Yes. If she'd found out he was alive, she'd have to grieve his death a second time."

"You might want to leave that part out," Max suggested.

Fiona grinned. "I will use the utmost discretion and tact."

"That'll be a first," muttered Teresa.

Fiona turned to her. "What was that?"

"I said you go first." Teresa stood up and gestured toward the door. "After you, dear sister." She followed Fiona through the door and turned back to give them a wink. "Lock up if you leave, will you?"

Eric leapt to his feet. "I almost forgot! I need to get back to my shop and pronto."

"Let me guess," Max said. "You left Daphne running the place and you want to get back before she burns it down."

"Or takes an order for a thousand peonies like she did last week. Do you know how hard it is to find peonies this time of year?" He leaned over and gave Max a kiss on the cheek and a fist bump to Keiko. "Stay out of trouble, you two."

Max and Keiko looked at each other. Keiko spoke first. "Now what?"

"I know what you're going to do," Max said. "You're going to get on your laptop, right?"

"I seem to have become too predictable."

"Not at all," Max assured her. "Reliable, yes. Predictable? Never. By the way, what was the big announcement that was supposed to happen the night of the murder? I don't know when I'm going to get a chance to ask my dad. Would you just tell me, please?"

"I don't know if I should." Keiko wiggled her eyebrows mischievously. "Okay, I'll tell you. It was two parts. First, Modern Artist magazine is doing a feature article about Richard, and one of his paintings will be on the cover."

"That's fantastic!" Max grinned. It felt good to hear some good news for a change. "What's the second part?"

"His show is, or rather was, being extended into

January," Keiko said. "Apparently, the pre-sales were way above expectations."

"Well, that's not going to happen now, obviously, but the magazine article will, right?"

"Yes," Keiko said. "It's coming out next month. What are you going to do while I'm researching?"

"I'm going to the police station and see if they'll let me talk to my dad." Max looked at her phone. "It's been almost an hour since the lawyer called me, and I'm getting worried."

"Tell him, well, you know," Keiko said, looking a bit embarrassed. "Tell him we love him."

"Will do."

CHAPTER 24

*M*ax meant to go straight to the police station, but when she drove past the Hildalgo Gallery, she thought a little detour might be in order.

Max had a theory that the killer threw the fedora and the duffle bag in a trash dumpster or stashed it in a bush nearby, rather than risk being caught with it. She figured they would have come back to get rid of the evidence, but what if Leo hadn't had the opportunity? He certainly couldn't go walking around in broad daylight if he were supposed to be dead.

Of course, the trash might have already been picked up by now, but it was still worth a look. If she found the duffle bag, the bust might be inside it with the murderer's fingerprints on it. Why else would the killer have taken it with them and shoved the other bust on the floor to make everyone think it was the murder weapon?

As soon as she saw the gallery on her left, she made a U-turn and pulled up in front. It appeared deserted. She didn't want to leave the bright red Mini Cooper parked in front where someone she knew might recognize it, so she drove around to the back and pulled into the alley.

A small, white van was backed up to the loading area behind the gallery. She drove forward slowly until she could see that it was a rented moving van. Was Henry moving paintings to another location? Maybe he had to be out of the space and was moving them into storage.

She was surprised to see Henry carrying something from the van into the gallery. She drove forward and pulled into one of the gallery spaces.

"Good morning, Henry," she called out when he re-emerged at the loading gate. "Have you decided to take over the gallery after all?"

Max couldn't understand the suspicious look he gave her until it occurred to her that he might have heard that her father had been arrested for Xavier's murder.

"I'm having one last show before I close it down for good," he said.

"Who's the artist?" she asked.

"I am."

"Really." She didn't know why she was surprised. He'd told her that Xavier was going to have a showing of his work. "That's wonderful, Henry. I'm glad you were able to go ahead with your show in spite of everything."

"My father would have wanted me to go through with it."

"I'm sure you're right," Max agreed. "It's a wonderful way to honor his memory."

Henry's face softened, and he showed the hint of a smile.

"There's something else," Max said. "I think I might know who killed your father, Henry."

His eyes narrowed but he didn't respond.

"Did you hear that Leo faked his own death? Apparently, when a well-known artist dies, the price of his work can go up quite a bit. Even double."

"Of course, I know that," he said. "So, Leo is alive, after all. And you think he killed my father?"

"I think so, but Leo isn't alive now. Eliana shot him last night. Accidentally," she added.

His eyes widened. "You're saying he didn't die in Mexico—he died last night?"

Max nodded and walked over to the back of the van to take a look at Henry's artwork. The van was full of junk. She really didn't understand the art world at all.

"They hated each other, you know," Henry said. "When Leo came to pick up his paintings, there were others my dad had in storage that he didn't tell him about. When he found out about the plane crash, he bragged about it and made me promise not to tell anyone. Maybe Leo found out."

"Maybe," Max said, and waited to see if Henry would tell her more.

"Yeah." Henry seemed to think this over. Maybe he was trying to remember what his dad had told him. "He figured no one would be the wiser, and later he could sell the paintings for twice what they were going for before."

"Would you mind if I tell the police what you've told me? They might want to talk to you. It would help a lot."

Henry didn't seem to hear her. "He must have been the guy your dad saw. The one with the fedora and the duffle bag."

"You know about that?"

"Yeah. The police told me." He pulled on a pair of work gloves before retrieving a mangled piece of metal from the back of the van. It must have been heavy, since he seemed to struggle with it.

"Can I help?" Max asked.

Henry merely grunted and shook his head, carrying the piece into the gallery. Max followed him inside.

Henry placed the bent hunk of barbed wire fence on a pedestal, which didn't help, as far as Max was concerned. Still, she wanted to stay on his good side, since she'd need his help to convince Detective Gallagher that Leo was the murderer and not her dad.

"That makes quite a statement," Max said, hoping her noncommittal comment would be taken positively. "Do you title your artwork?"

"This is Calamity Number 7."

Max considered this. She'd spent enough time around her father and his artist friends. She should be able to fake it. "Yes, yes, I see it. That really captures the mood of this piece. So, is there a Calamity 1 through 6?"

Henry seemed pleased by her attempt at flattery. "My creative process works non-linearly. There is a Calamity number 3, but we'll have to see if there will be more. I'm in a more positive mental space now. My latest work is Possibility number 17. Would you like to see it?"

"Yes, I would," Max said, surprised that she felt curiosity about his work. Maybe if she saw more of his pieces, it would all start to make sense. "But first I'm going to go out back and see if I can find anything in the dumpsters or bushes."

"You won't find anything," he said. "The trash truck came yesterday."

"Darn." Max had expected this, but the disappointment hit her hard. "I'll look through the shrubs at least." She headed for the back door even though she had little hope of finding anything. She still had to try.

"The police did that, you know. They didn't find the hat or the bust."

Max froze in her tracks but didn't turn to look at Henry. "The what?"

Henry was quiet for several seconds. "The hat and the duffle bag."

Max took a deep breath to compose herself and stared at the floor which was strewn with fliers. "Oh, right." She hadn't mentioned her theory that the duffle bag held another bust to the police. Did they have the same theory, and had they shared the information with Henry? It seemed unlikely.

"It would have been stupid to leave it laying around for the police to find, don't you think?"

Henry's words sent a chill down Max's spine. She did her best to control her voice, and not to show the alarm she felt building inside her. "I guess there's no point in looking then. You'll need to sweep up before your big night." She hoped her voice sounded light-hearted, as she bent down and picked up one of the fliers. It featured the shows that Xavier had planned for the next two months. Henry's name wasn't on the schedule.

"Why the rush?" Henry followed her to the back door.

"I was just on my way to visit my dad," she said, willing herself not to look back. If she could just get out the door, she'd be fine. "He'll start to worry if I don't get there soon."

She didn't make it to the back door first. Henry swept past her and stood between her and the exit.

"No need to rush off, Max," he said. "I could use some help setting up my displays." There was a pile of junk just inside the loading dock, and he picked up a hunk of twisted metal.

His voice sounded menacing, or perhaps it was just her imagination. Was it possible that Henry had killed his own father?

At that moment, all the pieces clicked into place. Henry was the person who was in the wrong place. It was Henry who put on his father's fedora and slipped out the back door. He would have had plenty of time to stash the hat and duffle bag and walk down the alley and around to the front entrance. Then, all he had to do was light up a cigarette and wait for Xavier's body to be discovered.

Max felt her heart pound and began to feel light-headed. How was she going to get out of this one? Henry stood between her and the open loading dock, and on her right was the cabinet she knew hid the corridor to the second back door.

The metal piece of junk he held had to weigh ten pounds and could easily knock her out and possibly kill her, just like Xavier had been killed with the bust. The only thing Max could think to do was to stall until she thought of something better.

"Why did you do it?" she asked. "Was it because he wouldn't give you your own show?"

Henry seemed to deflate before her eyes. "He said he had a reputation, and he couldn't destroy everything he'd worked for by putting my artwork in his gallery. He laughed at me!"

"That's terrible, Henry. Maybe he just doesn't understand art the way you do."

That got his attention, and she saw a hopeful look in his eyes, as if he'd finally met a true believer. But it didn't last. "You're just saying that, so I don't kill you, too."

Max heard a soft click from the corridor behind her. It sounded like someone opening the second door.

"But why would you kill me?" She hoped her voice covered up the sound of whoever had just opened the secret door. It was always tricky to reason with a madman, but she had to buy time. "All I care about is getting my dad out of jail. With your help, we can pin the murder on Leo. If I'm dead, there's no way you can have your show."

"I'll have a show somewhere else," Henry said, adjusting the heavy metal sculpture to get a better grasp of it.

Max didn't take her eyes off Henry as she took a step aside away from the cabinet, hoping the police were about to crash through and save the day.

"Don't move," Henry hissed, and raised the sculpture over his head as if to fling it at her.

At that moment, the cabinet toppled over, and Henry jumped out of the way. Max took advantage of his distraction and gave him a good shove.

Henry cried out in pain as he landed on the pile of scrap metal, wire, and other sharp, pointy objects and then lay motionless.

Max turned to see Keiko climb around the fallen cabinet.

"That must hurt," Keiko said as she pulled out her phone.

"I sure am glad to see you," Max said with a grin. "You have amazing timing."

"Someone has to keep you out of trouble," Keiko

said. "With Jason on his way to Miami, I guess I have to fill in." She spoke into the phone. "There's been an accident. Send the paramedics and the police."

Max took her eyes off Henry and turned to Keiko. "What made you come here? I thought you were doing research at the Knitpickers."

"And I thought you were going to the police station to see your dad," Keiko scolded. "When I saw that you had stopped here, I started to worry."

"You saw I stopped here? How did you know that? Are you tracking my phone?"

"No," Keiko said sheepishly. "Not your phone."

Max thought for a moment before it came to her. "My jacket?" She couldn't believe Keiko's beautiful present had a tracker. "How could you do such a thing without telling me?"

"It wouldn't be a very good test if I had told you."

Max's curiosity got the better of her. "A test?"

"I thought it would be helpful to be able to track certain people."

"Certain people like your friends?" Max asked, still indignant.

"Of course not." Keiko grinned. "But when I finished the jacket, it seemed like a good opportunity to see how well a tracker might work if we needed to use one in the future."

Sirens sounded in the distance, and they both watched Henry to see if he would regain consciousness.

"Is he dead?" Keiko asked.

Max moved closer to Henry, but not too close. She watched his chest until she saw a slight movement from shallow breathing. "He's alive, but he's going to be in a lot of pain when he comes to."

"Good," Keiko said.

CHAPTER 25

*M*ax pushed open the door to her dad's studio. He stared at the unfinished painting of the beautiful, Bolivian woman she now knew was Eliana.

"It's a beautiful painting," she said. "Are you going to finish it?"

"I'm not sure," he said. "Maybe someday."

"Sorry it didn't work out with her," Max said. "I know you really cared about her. And I think she cared about you, too."

"Not as much as she cares about money," he said. "As soon as she found the key to the storage space with all Leo's paintings, she was on a plane home."

"At least now we know why Leo tried to break into Eliana's house. I'm guessing he lost the second key. He must have been going nuts, making such a stupid mistake."

"I'd rather not talk about Eliana," Richard said. "Or Leo."

Max walked over to his side and put a hand on his shoulder, giving it a gentle squeeze. "Which is why you should come join us for pizza. Everyone's asking for you. Teresa and Simon brought champagne."

"I don't really feel much like celebrating," he said. "Don't get me wrong, I'm grateful that Henry's in jail, and I'm out. It's just—"

"There's beer, too. Fiona brought it," she said. "Non-celebratory, regular everyday beer. You know, what you drink when you hang out with your friends just to be sociable. Oliva and Zach are here too. And Keiko brought sushi."

"Of course, she did." He smiled. "Maybe I'll join you in a bit."

"Isn't Richard joining us?" Teresa asked when Max returned to the living room. "Simon and I have an announcement to make."

"He might join us later," Max said. "What is it?"

"Hold on," Fiona said. She walked down the hall to the studio. "Richard, you come out here. Teresa and Simon have something to say."

Richard followed Fiona back to the living room, and Teresa handed him a glass of champagne.

Simon spoke. "I would like to propose a toast, to a wonderful group of friends, and especially to my beautiful fiancé."

"Here, here," Max said, as everyone clinked glasses.

"Go on," Teresa said, tapping Simon's arm.

"We're ready to set a date." When everyone started talking excitedly, he raised his hands. "We need your help to pick the right date." He looked around the room. "What is everyone doing next Saturday?"

"Saturday!" Fiona exclaimed. "But that doesn't give me enough time to arrange everything."

"Life's too short, Fiona," Teresa said. "And we're not getting any younger. So, no arguments. It will be small and simple, but I want everyone in this room to be there."

Richard walked over and stood next to Max. "At least someone's love life is going as planned."

Max turned and saw he was smiling. "At least we have each other."

Richard gestured to the room full of friends, laughing and eating pizza. "Not to mention all of these characters."

"You got that right."

Teresa asked Max, "Where is your nice young man?"

"You mean Jason?" Max smiled at Teresa, trying to ignore the pang in her heart when she said his name out loud. "He's on his way to Miami. Looks like he's moving there."

Teresa's eyes widened. "Without you?"

"He asked me to go with him, but if there's one thing I know for sure, it's that I belong right here. For now, anyway."

The doorbell rang and Richard went to answer it.

Teresa sighed. "And here I thought you two were meant for each other."

Max turned when she heard an unexpected voice and saw Jason standing in the doorway.

"Come in," Richard said. "The more the merrier."

"I'm here to see Max," Jason said.

"I thought you were on a plane to Miami," Max said, confused.

Jason took a few tentative steps toward her. "I couldn't go without you," he said. "I rescheduled my flight, and I bought another ticket for you."

"I'm sorry, Jason," Max said, willing her heart to stop pounding in her chest. "I told you I don't want to move to Miami."

"Just let me finish, please," he said. "I got you a ticket, and then I stopped by to see my abuelita—my grandmother—and came straight here. I want you to come with me and meet my parents."

"But, Jason," Max began, ready to explain again why she didn't want to move.

Jason took both of her hands and held them gently. "I want you to meet my parents and then come back to Crystal Shores with me and marry me."

"What?" Max looked around the room, trying to figure out what was happening.

"I love this crazy town. I love all these people." Jason swept his arm around the room. "But most of all, I love you."

Max stopped breathing as he got down on one knee and took something out of his pocket. "My abuelita has been keeping this for me since the day I was born, and we both think you should have it." He held up a white gold ring set with sparkling diamonds. "Max, would you marry me?"

"But Miami... your new job." Max looked into his eyes trying to make sense of everything. This morning he was leaving her, possibly forever. And now?

"I have a job," Jason said. "Right here. All I'm missing is you. Marry me."

The room was silent, and time seemed to have stopped, until Max found the words to speak.

"Of course, I'll marry you."

Jason leapt up and threw his arms around her as the others hooted and hollered.

Teresa leaned over to Fiona and whispered. "We could make it a double wedding."

Thank you for reading Murder in Lavender Silk! Next up—Murder in Pink Taffeta, the long-awaited final novel in the series.

MURDER IN PINK TAFFETA

There's revenge, betrayal, and a murder to solve before Max can finally walk down the aisle with her handsome detective fiancé.

And if that wasn't enough, someone is doing their best to sabotage the wedding.

Will Max finally get her happy-ever-after ending?

Get Murder in Pink Taffeta and find out!

Join Karen's Cozy Club on my website: www.karensuewalker.com. I'll do my best to entertain and inspire you along with informing you about giveaways, freebies, and new releases.

For lots of fun stuff, follow me on Facebook at www.facebook.com/bridalshopmysteries or on Instagram at https://www.instagram.com/karensuewalker_author

Have a question or just want to say hi? Email me at karen@karensuewalker.com.

Made in United States
North Haven, CT
18 January 2026

86912338R00143